The Hidden Gem

Kishan Heraman

Published by Kishan Heraman, 2024.

THE HIDDEN GEM

First edition. August 22, 2024.

ISBN: 979-8227940735

Written by Kishan Heraman.

Table of Contents

To all the readers of *The Hidden Gem*,

Thank you for embarking on this journey with Nicholas and Zhoha. Your support and enthusiasm bring this story to life in ways I could only imagine.

A special note of gratitude goes to Zayn Jamshaid, whose remarkable work, *Cracked Reflection*, has been a profound inspiration for me. Zayn's storytelling and creativity encouraged me to explore my own imagination and dive into the world of writing. This book is a testament to the spark you ignited in me.

To everyone who has picked up this novel, your interest means the world to me. I hope you find as much magic and wonder in these pages as I did in crafting them.

With heartfelt thanks, Kishan Heraman.

Chapter 1: Serenity in Brooksville

Nicholas Burgess had always found peace in the quiet corners of Brooksville, a small town with a timeless charm. On this chilly autumn afternoon, he walked through the town's cobblestone streets, where the trees had shed their summer green in favour of vibrant shades of red, orange, and gold. The crisp air was filled with the sound of crunching leaves beneath his shoes, and he enjoyed the way the cool breeze ruffled his hair.

Nicholas had a routine of taking solitary walks like this, enjoying the calm and the opportunity to clear his mind. Today, his stroll took him past a row of quaint shops, each one more charming than the last. But it was the old bookstore nestled between two modern stores that caught his eye. Its faded sign and ivy-covered walls spoke of history and mystery, standing in stark contrast to the newer, glossier establishments around it.

Intrigued, Nicholas pushed open the heavy wooden door. It creaked on its hinges, announcing his arrival with a nostalgic groan. Inside, the store was a treasure trove of forgotten books. Shelves lined the walls, stacked high with volumes of every shape and size. The air was thick with the scent of aged paper and leather, a comforting aroma that promised the presence of countless stories waiting to be discovered.

Nicholas wandered through the narrow aisles, his fingers grazing the spines of the books as he moved. Each title was a potential adventure, a portal to a different world. As he made his way through the labyrinth of shelves, he came across a high shelf where an old book rested. It was bound in cracked leather, its cover worn and faded with age. The title was barely legible, obscured by time and neglect.

Feeling a surge of curiosity, Nicholas reached up to take the book down. As he carefully pulled it from the shelf, he couldn't help but marvel at its age and the mysteries it might hold. The book was heavy in his hands, its cover adorned with intricate but nearly erased designs. He opened it slowly, revealing pages that were yellowed and delicate, filled with handwritten notes and faded illustrations. Nicholas's heart raced with excitement at the thought of uncovering the secrets within.

Just then, the bell above the door jingled again. Nicholas looked up, his attention momentarily pulled away from the book. In walked a girl who seemed like a breath of fresh air in the musty bookstore. She had an adventurous spirit about her, evident from the way her dark hair was tied back in a practical ponytail and the curious glint in her eyes. Her gaze immediately fell on Nicholas, who was still holding the old book.

"Hey, what's that you've got there?" she asked, her voice friendly but tinged with an unmistakable hint of intrigue.

Nicholas looked up, startled by her sudden appearance. "I'm not sure," he said, his voice a mix of wonder and uncertainty. "It looks like it's been here for ages. I was just about to see what it's all about."

The girl's eyes widened with interest. "Can I take a look?" she asked, her enthusiasm palpable. "I love finding old books like this. They always have such interesting stories."

Nicholas nodded, handing her the book with a smile. "Sure. I'd love to hear what you think."

As she took the book, her fingers lightly brushed against Nicholas's. She opened it carefully, her eyes scanning the pages with a mixture of curiosity and excitement. "This is fascinating," she said after a moment. "It looks like it might be something special. I love the way old books hold onto their mysteries."

Nicholas nodded in agreement, feeling a sense of camaraderie in their shared enthusiasm. "I've always felt that way too. There's something magical about uncovering a story that's been hidden away for so long."

The girl's face lit up with a warm smile. "I'm Zhoha, by the way. I'm new in town and just exploring. This bookstore is amazing. I'm glad I found it."

"I'm Nicholas," he said, extending a hand. "Nice to meet you. If you're looking for more interesting books, I'd be happy to show you around."

Zhoha's smile widened. "That would be great. I'm always on the lookout for unique finds. Let's see what else this place has to offer."

Nicholas led Zhoha through the store, pointing out various sections and sharing some of his favourite books. As they walked, they fell into an easy conversation about their shared love for literature. They discussed their favourite genres, authors, and stories, finding joy in their mutual interests. Nicholas was pleasantly surprised by how comfortable he felt with Zhoha. Her enthusiasm and curiosity were infectious, making their exploration of the bookstore even more enjoyable.

They discovered that they had a lot in common. Both loved the idea of uncovering hidden gems and enjoyed the thrill of discovering new stories. Their conversation flowed naturally, and they quickly found themselves discussing everything from classic novels to obscure historical texts. Nicholas was impressed by Zhoha's knowledge and her genuine passion for books. It was refreshing to meet someone who shared his interests so deeply.

As they continued to browse, Nicholas led Zhoha to a cosy corner of the store where a few comfortable chairs were nestled among stacks of books. They settled into the chairs, continuing their conversation about their favourite reads and authors. The warm light from a nearby lamp cast a soft glow over their faces, and the quiet hum of the store provided a peaceful backdrop to their discussion.

"This place is incredible," Zhoha said, her eyes shining with excitement. "It feels like a treasure chest of stories waiting to be discovered. I'm so glad I found it."

Nicholas nodded, feeling a sense of satisfaction. "I'm glad you did too. It's not everyday you meet someone who shares your love for books and adventure."

As the afternoon wore on, Nicholas and Zhoha found themselves deeply engrossed in their conversation. They laughed about their favourite literary characters and debated the merits of different genres. Nicholas felt a sense of connection with Zhoha that he hadn't experienced before. Her presence was a breath of fresh air, and he found himself opening up in ways he rarely did with others.

Eventually, it was time for Zhoha to leave. She gathered her things, and Nicholas walked her to the door. As she stepped out into the crisp autumn air, she turned back with a smile. "This has been really fun. I'm glad we met and had the chance to explore the bookstore together."

Nicholas felt a pang of disappointment at her departure but was also excited about the new friendship they had formed. "Me too. I've enjoyed our time together. If you're ever looking for more book recommendations or just want to hang out, let me know."

Zhoha nodded. "I'd like that. I'm sure we'll have plenty more adventures ahead."

As Zhoha walked away, Nicholas watched her disappear into the distance. He felt a sense of anticipation and excitement about what the future might hold. The book they had discovered together was just the beginning of something new and intriguing.

In the days that followed, Nicholas and Zhoha continued to stay in touch. They shared their thoughts on books they had read and discussed new discoveries. Their friendship grew stronger as they explored different parts of Brooksville and delved into their shared passion for literature.

One evening, while browsing through an old book of local legends at the bookstore, Nicholas stumbled upon something unexpected. Hidden within the pages was a faded map, depicting an ancient treasure buried somewhere in Willow Creek. The map was old and worn, but it was clear enough to show that the treasure was rumoured to be a gem of immense beauty and power.

Nicholas's heart raced with excitement as he examined the map. He couldn't wait to show it to Zhoha and share the adventure with her. The idea of uncovering a hidden treasure in their small town seemed like a perfect continuation of their newfound friendship.

He reached out to Zhoha, and they made plans to meet at the bookstore to discuss the map. As they prepared for their next adventure, Nicholas couldn't shake the feeling that this was just the beginning of something extraordinary. The hidden gem was waiting to be discovered, and with Zhoha by his side, he felt ready to embark on the quest that lay ahead.

Chapter 2: Adventurous

Weeks passed, and Nicholas and Zhoha's friendship grew stronger with each shared adventure. Their days were filled with exploration, whether it was unearthing the secrets of Brooksville's hidden nooks or simply enjoying the charm of its local eateries and parks. Each moment they spent together seemed to strengthen their bond, as if their connection was woven tighter with every new experience.

One cool autumn evening, as the golden hues of sunset filtered through the dusty windows of the quaint Brooksville bookstore, Nicholas and Zhoha found themselves immersed in their latest hobby: delving into the town's rich tapestry of local legends. The store was a treasure trove of old maps, antique books, and curious artefacts, each item holding stories from a bygone era.

Nicholas had always been fascinated by the bookstore's charm. Its creaky wooden floors, the musty scent of old paper, and the warmth of its dimly lit aisles created an atmosphere ripe for discovery. It was on one of these particular evenings, while rummaging through a neglected section of the store dedicated to local history, that Nicholas stumbled upon something extraordinary.

The book was an ancient, leather-bound tome with gold embossed lettering that read "The Legends of Brooksville." Its pages were yellowed with age and filled with intricate illustrations and tales of long-forgotten events. Nicholas's fingers traced the faded script as he flipped through the pages, his eyes catching on a map tucked between two sections. The map was old, its edges frayed and corners curling, but it was the drawing that captured his attention: a sketch of Willow Creek with strange symbols marking a specific location.

Nicholas's heart raced with excitement as he realised the significance of what he had found. The map seemed to indicate the presence of a hidden treasure, an ancient gem buried somewhere in the heart of Willow Creek. He called Zhoha over, his enthusiasm barely contained. Her eyes widened with intrigue as she examined the map.

"This looks like an adventure waiting to happen," she said, her voice tinged with excitement. Her gaze shifted from the map to Nicholas, the thrill of the discovery reflected in her eyes.

Nicholas nodded vigorously. "I think so too. This could be the adventure we've been looking for. What do you say we find out where this hidden gem is?"

Zhoha's smile widened, and she clapped her hands together in anticipation. "Absolutely. Let's do it!"

They spent the next few hours poring over the map, tracing the routes and landmarks it depicted. The map seemed to be a combination of old-world artistry and cryptic symbols, making it both captivating and challenging to decipher. Nicholas and Zhoha used every bit of their combined knowledge and intuition to interpret the clues. They marked the location on a modern map of Brooksville, trying to correlate the old landmarks with the current ones.

By the time they left the bookstore, it was late, and the streets of Brooksville were bathed in the soft glow of street lamps. The crisp night air was filled with a sense of possibility and excitement. Nicholas and Zhoha agreed to meet early the next morning to begin their quest. They parted ways, each brimming with anticipation for the adventure that awaited them.

The following morning, they met at the edge of Willow Creek, the starting point of their journey. The creek itself was a picturesque scene, with clear waters gently flowing over smooth stones and surrounded by lush greenery. The map's markings had led them here, and both felt a sense of anticipation as they stood on the banks of the creek, the air buzzing with the promise of discovery.

Nicholas and Zhoha followed the map's indications, which guided them along a path that wound through the dense forest on the creek's edge. The forest was a mosaic of colours, with autumn leaves creating a vibrant carpet beneath their feet. They navigated through the underbrush, their senses heightened as they searched for any sign of the gem's location.

Every so often, they would stop to examine a peculiar rock formation or a distinct tree that matched the landmarks on the map. Their conversations were punctuated by laughter and excited whispers as they uncovered various natural wonders and marvels along their path.

As they ventured deeper into the forest, the path became less distinct, and the terrain more rugged. The sun was beginning its descent, casting long shadows across their path. Just as they were about to consider turning back, Zhoha spotted something unusual—a large stone archway partially hidden by vines and moss.

"This must be it," she said, her voice filled with awe. The stone archway matched a distinctive feature on the map, and they could see faint, ancient symbols carved into its surface.

Nicholas and Zhoha carefully made their way through the archway, their hearts pounding with excitement. On the other side, the forest opened up to reveal a hidden grove, a serene clearing surrounded by towering trees. In the centre of the grove was an old stone pedestal, its surface covered in ivy and lichen.

At the base of the pedestal was a small, intricately carved box. The box was adorned with symbols that matched those on the map, and it seemed to be waiting for them. Nicholas and Zhoha exchanged glances, their excitement palpable as they approached the pedestal.

Nicholas reached out and carefully opened the box. Inside, nestled in a bed of velvet, was the hidden gem—an exquisite, shimmering stone that seemed to capture the light in a mesmerising way. Its surface was smooth and polished, and it radiated a subtle, otherworldly glow.

Zhoha's eyes were wide with wonder. "We found it. The hidden gem is real!"

Nicholas grinned, his heart swelling with pride and joy. "We did it! This is incredible."

As they stood there, marvelling at their discovery, a sense of accomplishment washed over them. Their journey had been filled with challenges and excitement, but the reward was beyond anything they had imagined. The gem was not just a physical treasure; it symbolised their shared adventure and the deepening of their friendship.

However, as they prepared to leave the grove, a sense of unease began to settle in. The shadows in the forest seemed to grow darker, and a chill in the air made them shiver. The serene beauty of the grove had taken on a different, more ominous tone.

Nicholas and Zhoha decided to return to Brooksville with the gem, their steps hurried as they retraced their path through the forest. The journey back felt more intense, as if they were being watched by unseen eyes. The forest, once welcoming and full of promise, now seemed to hold a quiet, enigmatic presence.

When they finally emerged from the forest and reached the safety of Brooksville, they breathed a sigh of relief. The town's familiar sights and sounds were a comforting contrast to the eerie atmosphere of the grove. They made their way to the bookstore to share their discovery with the owner, an elderly man with a deep knowledge of Brooksville's history and legends.

The bookstore owner listened with rapt attention as Nicholas and Zhoha recounted their adventure. When they presented the hidden gem, his eyes widened in recognition. He carefully examined the gem and then looked up at them with a mixture of curiosity and concern.

"This gem," he said slowly, "is indeed a significant find. It's said to be connected to an ancient legend about a powerful artefact hidden in the region. Many have sought it, but few have succeeded."

Nicholas and Zhoha exchanged glances, their curiosity piqued. "What's the legend?" Zhoha asked.

The bookstore owner hesitated, then began to recount a tale that had been passed down through generations. According to the legend, the gem was not just a beautiful object but a key to unlocking an ancient power hidden deep within the land. It was said that those who possessed the gem could unlock secrets long buried and potentially wield great influence.

"But," the owner added, "the gem's power is not to be taken lightly. There are stories of those who sought to misuse it, and their fates were far from favourable."

Nicholas and Zhoha listened intently, their excitement mingling with apprehension. The legend added a layer of complexity to their discovery, suggesting that the gem's significance extended beyond mere treasure.

As they left the bookstore, they felt a renewed sense of purpose. Their adventure had just begun, and the gem was only the first step in a journey that promised to reveal deeper secrets and challenges. The road ahead was uncertain, but they were ready to face whatever came next, driven by the thrill of discovery and the strength of their growing friendship.

Their next steps would involve delving deeper into the legend, unravelling the mysteries surrounding the gem, and understanding the ancient powers it was said to hold. Nicholas and Zhoha were poised on the brink of a new chapter in their adventure, one that would test their courage, intelligence, and bond as they continued their quest.

Chapter 3: Secrets Unveiled

Nicholas and Zhoha's discovery of the hidden gem had ignited a new spark of curiosity and excitement within them. The bookstore owner's tale about the gem's legendary power and the cautionary note about those who had sought to misuse it only deepened their resolve. As they walked away from the bookstore, their minds buzzed with questions and possibilities.

"It feels like we're on the brink of something huge," Zhoha said, her eyes reflecting the amber glow of the street lamps.

Nicholas nodded, his gaze fixed on the shimmering gem that he had carefully wrapped in a cloth. "Yeah, it's like we've uncovered the first piece of a much larger puzzle. We need to figure out what this power is all about and why it's so important."

They decided to head to Zhoha's house, where they could study the gem and the legend in more detail. Zhoha's home was a cosy, old-fashioned cottage on the outskirts of town, surrounded by a garden that was lush even in the late summer. As they entered, Zhoha's mother greeted them warmly, and Nicholas admired the house's charm—a mix of antique furniture and vibrant plants.

In the study, the two friends spread out their findings on the old oak table. The gem was now lying in the centre, its glow muted under the dim light of the desk lamp. Around it were the map, the ancient book, and several notepads filled with their observations and theories.

"I think we should start by researching the symbols on the gem and the map," Nicholas suggested, pointing to a detailed sketch of the symbols they had found. "They might give us clues about the gem's purpose."

Zhoha nodded, retrieving a magnifying glass from a nearby drawer. "Good idea. Let's compare these symbols with those in the book and see if we can find any matches or references."

For hours, they pored over the book, flipping through pages of faded illustrations and cryptic text. The symbols on the gem seemed to correspond with ancient runes and markings mentioned in the book. They discovered that the runes were associated with various elemental forces and were believed to be linked to powerful relics from ancient times.

"It's fascinating," Zhoha said, her eyes wide with intrigue. "These symbols are connected to different elements—earth, water, fire, and air. It's like the gem could be part of a larger set of artefacts."

Nicholas leaned back, considering this new information. "If this gem is one of a set, it might be that each piece holds a different aspect of the power mentioned in the legend. We need to find out if there are other gems or artefacts associated with this one."

Their research was interrupted by a sudden knock on the door. Zhoha's mother entered with a steaming pot of tea and a warm smile. "I thought you two might need a break. You've been at it for hours."

"Thanks, Mrs. Patel," Zhoha said, accepting the tea gratefully. "We've found some interesting things, but we still have a lot to figure out."

As they sipped their tea and discussed their findings, Nicholas's phone buzzed with a new message. It was from the bookstore owner, who had sent them a follow-up email with additional historical documents and records. Nicholas read the email aloud.

"The owner's sent over some old records related to Brooksville's history. It looks like there are references to other artefacts found in the area," Nicholas said, his voice tinged with excitement.

Zhoha's eyes sparkled. "Let's dive into these records and see if we can find any connections. This could be exactly what we need."

They spent the next few hours sifting through the digital records, cross-referencing dates, names, and locations. Slowly, a pattern began to emerge. There were mentions of other artefacts with similar symbols, found in various locations around Brooksville and its surrounding areas.

"This is incredible," Nicholas said. "It looks like Brooksville has been a focal point for these artefacts throughout history. If we can track down these other items, we might be able to unlock more about the gem's power."

Zhoha's excitement was palpable. "We should start by visiting the locations mentioned in the records. There might be clues or even more artefacts waiting to be discovered."

The next morning, Nicholas and Zhoha set out on their first field trip, armed with their notes and the historical records. Their first stop was an old mill on the edge of town, which, according to the records, had been the site of an excavation in the early 1900s. The mill had since fallen into disrepair, its once-bustling machinery now overgrown with vines and moss.

"This place looks like it's been abandoned for years," Nicholas said as they approached the old structure. "But there might be something here."

Zhoha scanned the area with a keen eye. "Let's start by looking around the grounds. There could be hidden compartments or old storage rooms that might have been overlooked."

They carefully explored the mill, searching for any signs of historical artefacts or hidden compartments. After an hour of sifting through debris and examining old machinery, they stumbled upon a small, locked room in the back of the building.

"This could be it," Zhoha said, her voice filled with anticipation. "Let's see if we can get inside."

Nicholas examined the lock, which looked ancient and rusty. With a bit of effort, he managed to pry it open with a crowbar they had brought along. The room was dusty but surprisingly well-preserved. Inside, they found old crates and boxes, many of which were marked with faded labels.

As they began to open the boxes, their excitement grew. Some of the boxes contained old tools and machinery parts, but one crate held a collection of old journals and maps. Nicholas carefully opened the journals, their pages yellowed and brittle with age.

"Look at this," Nicholas said, holding up a journal with a worn cover. "It looks like the owner of the mill kept detailed notes about the artefacts they found."

Zhoha peered over his shoulder. "These notes might give us more information about the artefacts and their locations."

The journals revealed detailed descriptions of several artefacts, including their appearances, locations, and the people who had found them. Among the entries was a mention of a small, intricately carved box that matched the one they had found in the grove.

"This box was found in a nearby cave," Zhoha said, reading aloud from the journal. "It's described as having similar symbols to the ones on our gem."

Nicholas's eyes lit up. "If this is the same box, it means we're on the right track. We need to visit this cave and see if there are any more artefacts or clues hidden there."

Their next destination was a cave system located about an hour's drive from Brooksville. As they approached the entrance, the cave loomed dark and foreboding, its entrance partially obscured by dense vegetation.

"This place feels eerie," Nicholas said, his voice echoing in the cavern's mouth. "But we've come this far. Let's see what we can find."

With flashlights in hand, they ventured into the cave, their footsteps echoing off the damp walls. The air was cool and musty, and the cave's depths seemed to stretch endlessly. They followed the notes from the journal, which described a series of tunnels and chambers.

After navigating several twists and turns, they finally reached a chamber that matched the description from the journal. In the centre of the chamber was an old stone pedestal, similar to the one in the grove.

"Here it is," Zhoha said, her voice filled with awe. "This must be the location described in the journal."

On the pedestal was another small, carved box. It was almost identical to the one they had found but with a different set of symbols. Nicholas carefully opened it, revealing another artefact—a small, ornate amulet with intricate designs.

"This amulet is beautiful," Nicholas said, examining it closely. "And it matches the symbols from the journal."

Zhoha took a deep breath, her excitement evident. "We're finding pieces of a larger puzzle. Each artefact might be linked to the others, and together they could unlock the secrets of the gem."

As they left the cave, the sun was beginning to set, casting long shadows across the landscape. Nicholas and Zhoha felt a deep sense of accomplishment and anticipation. They had uncovered more pieces of the puzzle, and the adventure was only just beginning.

Back at Zhoha's house, they laid out their new findings alongside the previous artefacts. The collection was growing, and with each discovery, the mystery surrounding the gem and its power became more intricate and compelling.

"We're making progress," Nicholas said, his eyes scanning the growing collection. "But there's still so much we don't know. We need to keep searching and connecting the dots."

Zhoha nodded, her gaze determined. "We've come this far, and we're not stopping now. There are more secrets to uncover and more adventures ahead."

As the evening settled in, Nicholas and Zhoha felt a renewed sense of purpose. The echoes of the past were calling them, and they were ready to answer. The journey ahead promised to be filled with challenges and discoveries, and they were eager to embrace every moment of it.

Their quest to unlock the gem's secrets had only just begun, and with each step, they were forging a path into the heart of an ancient mystery, guided by their friendship and an unyielding curiosity.

Chapter 4: Shadow's Embrace

The days that followed were a whirlwind of activity for Nicholas and Zhoha. Their discovery of the amulet in the cave had only fueled their curiosity and determination. Each new artefact they uncovered seemed to bring them closer to unravelling the mysteries of the hidden gem, but it also deepened the complexity of their quest.

Nicholas and Zhoha devoted their time to analysing the amulet and the symbols on it. They discovered that the amulet contained inscriptions that were remarkably similar to the runes on the gem, but with additional elements that hinted at a connection between them.

"We're building a picture here," Nicholas said one afternoon as they sat in Zhoha's study, surrounded by their growing collection of artefacts and documents. "These symbols seem to be part of a larger language or code. Each piece might be a part of an intricate puzzle."

Zhoha nodded in agreement, her eyes fixed on the amulet. "If these artefacts are connected, then there might be a way to decipher the full meaning of the symbols and understand the true power of the gem. But we need more pieces of the puzzle."

Their next step was to identify potential locations where other artefacts might be hidden. The records they had gathered from the mill mentioned several other sites around Brooksville that had been associated with similar artefacts. Determined to follow these leads, Nicholas and Zhoha planned their next expedition.

One of the locations mentioned was an old, abandoned chapel situated on the outskirts of Brooksville. The chapel had once been a place of significance in the town but had long since fallen into disuse. According to the records, it had been the site of a significant find in the early 1800s.

The chapel was located in a secluded area, surrounded by dense woods and overgrown with vegetation. As Nicholas and Zhoha approached the chapel, its weathered stone walls and crumbling steeple gave it an air of faded grandeur.

"This place looks like it's seen better days," Zhoha remarked as they pushed open the heavy wooden doors, which creaked ominously.

Inside, the chapel was dark and musty. Dust motes danced in the narrow beams of sunlight filtering through broken stained-glass windows. The interior was a mix of ancient pews, decaying tapestries, and a large, empty altar at the front.

Nicholas and Zhoha began their search in the chapel's main area. They carefully examined the altar and the surrounding space, looking for any signs of hidden compartments or clues.

"Let's check the basement," Nicholas suggested after a while. "The records mentioned that there were additional finds in the chapel's lower levels."

They found a narrow staircase leading down to a dark, subterranean chamber. As they descended, the air grew cooler and mustier. The basement was a labyrinth of stone walls and old storage rooms. Their flashlights cast eerie shadows on the walls as they explored.

In one of the rooms, they discovered a large, dust-covered chest. The chest was adorned with intricate carvings and had a heavy iron lock. Nicholas and Zhoha exchanged excited glances.

"This could be it," Zhoha said, her voice filled with anticipation. "Let's see if we can open it."

With some effort, Nicholas managed to pry open the lock. Inside the chest were several old manuscripts and a small, ornate box. The manuscripts were filled with detailed sketches and descriptions of artefacts, including some that matched the symbols they had been studying.

Nicholas carefully opened the small box, revealing another artefact: a beautifully crafted dagger with runes etched along the blade.

"This is incredible," Nicholas said, examining the dagger. "It matches the symbols we've been seeing. It looks like each artefact has a unique design but follows a common theme."

Zhoha's eyes shone with excitement. "This dagger could be another piece of the puzzle. We need to understand how it fits in with the other artefacts."

They spent the next few hours meticulously documenting their findings and taking detailed notes on the manuscripts. The manuscripts described various artefacts and their significance, suggesting that each item was part of a larger set of relics that held ancient power.

As they left the chapel, the sun was setting, casting a golden glow over the landscape. The air was crisp and cool, and a sense of accomplishment and anticipation filled them.

"We've found another crucial piece," Nicholas said as they drove back to Brooksville. "But I have a feeling there's more out there. We need to keep searching."

Back at Zhoha's house, they laid out the new artefacts alongside the previous ones. The collection was becoming impressive, but the complexity of the symbols and their meanings was growing.

"Each artefact seems to hold a unique power or significance," Zhoha observed, her brow furrowed in concentration. "If we can decipher their combined meaning, we might unlock the full potential of the hidden gem."

Their research was interrupted by a sudden knock on the door. Zhoha's mother entered with a concerned look on her face.

"There's someone here to see you," she said. "He says it's urgent."

Nicholas and Zhoha exchanged puzzled glances. They followed Zhoha's mother to the front door, where a tall, sharply dressed man stood. His presence was commanding, and he carried an air of authority.

"Are you Nicholas and Zhoha?" the man asked, his voice smooth and professional.

"Yes, we are," Nicholas replied. "Can we help you?"

The man introduced himself as Mr. Langley, a historian with a particular interest in ancient artefacts. He explained that he had been following their progress and was intrigued by their discoveries.

"I've been researching similar artefacts for years," Mr. Langley said. "Your findings are remarkable, and I believe we might be able to help each other."

Nicholas and Zhoha were intrigued by Mr. Langley's offer. They invited him in and showed him their collection of artefacts. Mr. Langley examined each piece carefully, his expression one of deep concentration.

"This is impressive," Mr. Langley said finally. "You've uncovered artefacts that are believed to be part of an ancient collection. Each piece holds a fragment of a larger power, but together, they form a key to a long-forgotten secret."

Zhoha's curiosity was piqued. "What do you know about this secret?"

Mr. Langley took a deep breath. "The artefacts you've found are believed to be linked to a powerful relic known as the 'Heart of the Elements.' According to legend, this relic holds the combined power of all the elemental forces and can unlock incredible potential. However, it is also said that it must be used with great care."

Nicholas and Zhoha listened intently, their excitement growing.

"If this relic is real," Nicholas said, "then we're on the right path. How can we find it?"

Mr. Langley's gaze grew serious. "The Heart of the Elements is hidden in a place that is both sacred and protected. It is said to be concealed in a location known only to a few, and those who seek it must prove themselves worthy."

Zhoha's expression was a mix of determination and excitement. "We're ready to face whatever challenges lie ahead. We've come this far, and we're not stopping now."

Mr. Langley nodded approvingly. "I believe you're on the right track. The clues you've uncovered so far are significant, but there are still many pieces to the puzzle. We need to gather more information and continue our search."

As the night deepened, Nicholas, Zhoha, and Mr. Langley continued their discussion, planning their next steps in their quest. The journey ahead promised to be filled with new challenges and discoveries, but with each step, they felt their resolve strengthening.

The search for the Heart of the Elements was far from over, and the path ahead was shrouded in mystery. But with their combined knowledge and determination, Nicholas and Zhoha were ready to embrace the unknown and face the challenges that lay ahead. Guided by their friendship and an unyielding curiosity, they were prepared to uncover the secrets of the past and unlock the power of the hidden gem.

Chapter 5: Newfound Powers & Secrets

Nicholas and Zhoha awoke the next morning with a renewed sense of purpose. The revelation about the Heart of the Elements from Mr. Langley had invigorated their quest, but it also introduced a new layer of complexity. The idea of a sacred, protected location filled them with both anticipation and trepidation. The journey to uncover the full extent of the hidden gem's power was becoming increasingly daunting.

Their first order of business was to review the manuscripts and artefacts they had gathered. Mr. Langley had suggested that the information they had might contain clues about the Heart's location, so they needed to scrutinise every detail.

Sitting in Zhoha's study, surrounded by their collection, Nicholas and Zhoha worked diligently. They spread out the manuscripts, artefacts, and their notes across the large oak table. The amulet, dagger, and gem lay in the centre, their enigmatic symbols casting faint reflections in the dim light.

"This is a lot to process," Zhoha said, rubbing her temples as she scanned through the manuscripts. "But if there's a pattern or a hidden message, we need to find it."

Nicholas nodded, his eyes focused on a sketch of an ancient map that they had found in the chest. "The map might be the key. It seems to show various locations tied to the artefacts. If we can pinpoint the exact locations mentioned, we might find a pattern that leads us to the Heart of the Elements."

As they examined the map, a thought occurred to Nicholas. "What if the artefacts are leading us to a specific location, not just randomly scattered sites?"

Zhoha's eyes lit up. "That's a good point. We should try to connect the dots between the locations mentioned in the manuscripts and the map. Maybe there's a trail we're supposed to follow."

Their focus intensified as they worked together, plotting the locations from the map onto a digital map on Zhoha's laptop. The process was meticulous, but slowly, patterns began to emerge. Several sites seemed to form a rough circle around a central point, which appeared to be a region of dense forest.

"This central point could be the key," Nicholas said. "It might be where we need to focus our search."

Zhoha agreed, her fingers hovering over the keyboard. "If the Heart of the Elements is hidden somewhere in this forest, we need to gather more information about it. We should look for any historical records or local legends related to this area."

As they prepared for their next expedition, Zhoha's mother brought in a fresh batch of tea, offering them words of encouragement. "Be careful out there, you two. Sometimes the search for ancient secrets can be more dangerous than it seems."

With their supplies packed and their route mapped out, Nicholas and Zhoha set out towards the forested area. The journey was scenic but uneventful until they reached the edge of the forest. The dense trees and undergrowth created an atmosphere of foreboding, and a chill seemed to settle in the air.

"This place feels different," Nicholas remarked, his voice tinged with unease. "Like it's hiding something."

Zhoha nodded, her eyes scanning the dense foliage. "We should stay alert. The map suggests that there might be hidden paths or markers we need to look for."

They ventured into the forest, following a narrow, overgrown trail. The trees were tall and ancient, their gnarled branches casting deep shadows on the forest floor. As they walked, the sounds of the outside world faded away, replaced by the eerie silence of the forest.

After several hours of hiking, they reached a clearing with an old stone structure in the centre. It was partially overgrown with ivy, but its intricate carvings and arches were still visible.

"This must be it," Zhoha said, her voice echoing slightly in the clearing. "The structure matches descriptions from the manuscripts."

Nicholas approached the structure, examining the carvings. They resembled the runes and symbols they had seen on the artefacts. "These symbols are similar to those on the gem and the dagger. It looks like we've found another clue."

The structure appeared to be a small temple or shrine, and in the centre was a pedestal with a shallow basin. The basin was empty, but it seemed to be a focal point of the structure.

"Do you think there's something we're supposed to place here?" Nicholas asked, studying the pedestal.

Zhoha thought for a moment. "It could be. Maybe we need to use one of the artefacts to reveal a hidden mechanism or message."

They decided to test this theory, carefully placing the gem on the pedestal. As they did, a soft rumbling sound filled the air, and the pedestal began to glow with a faint light.

Zhoha gasped. "It's reacting to the gem!"

The light from the pedestal grew brighter, and a hidden compartment in the pedestal's base slowly revealed itself. Inside the compartment was an old scroll, sealed with a wax emblem that matched the symbols they had been studying.

Nicholas carefully unrolled the scroll, revealing a set of instructions and a map with more detailed markings. The instructions described a ritual that needed to be performed to unlock the power of the artefacts and reveal the Heart of the Elements.

"This scroll is a guide," Nicholas said, his voice filled with awe. "It tells us how to use the artefacts to find the Heart."

The instructions detailed a series of steps that involved aligning the artefacts with specific symbols in the forest and performing a ritual at the central point of the map.

"We need to follow these steps," Zhoha said, her eyes wide with determination. "This might be our chance to uncover the Heart of the Elements."

They spent the next few hours following the instructions, aligning the artefacts with the symbols marked on the scroll and performing the ritual as described. The process was intricate and required precise coordination.

As they completed the final step, a soft glow emanated from the central point of the map, and a hidden passageway began to open in the ground. The entrance to the passageway was concealed by thick vines and foliage, but it now revealed a dark, descending staircase.

"This is it," Nicholas said, his voice filled with a mix of excitement and apprehension. "We've found the way to the Heart of the Elements."

Zhoha took a deep breath, her gaze steady. "Let's proceed with caution. We don't know what we might encounter down there."

With flashlights in hand, Nicholas and Zhoha descended the staircase into the darkness. The air grew cooler and more humid as they moved deeper underground. The passageway was narrow, and the walls were lined with ancient carvings that depicted scenes of elemental forces and powerful relics.

After what felt like an eternity, they reached a large chamber with a high ceiling. The chamber was illuminated by a soft, ethereal light that seemed to emanate from a pedestal in the centre. On the pedestal was a large, ornate chest, adorned with intricate symbols and carvings.

"This must be it," Zhoha said, her voice echoing in the chamber. "The Heart of the Elements has to be inside that chest."

Nicholas approached the pedestal, his heart pounding with anticipation. He carefully opened the chest, revealing a dazzling array of artefacts, each one more ornate and intricate than the last. In the centre of the chest was a large, glowing crystal, its light pulsing with a rhythmic energy.

"This is incredible," Nicholas said, his voice filled with awe. "We've found the Heart of the Elements."

The crystal's glow seemed to resonate with the artefacts they had collected, and a sense of unity and power filled the chamber. Nicholas and Zhoha stood in reverent silence, absorbing the magnitude of their discovery.

As they examined the artefacts and the crystal, a sudden, cold draft swept through the chamber. The air grew heavy, and shadows seemed to dance on the walls. An ominous presence filled the chamber, and Nicholas and Zhoha exchanged uneasy glances.

"We're not alone," Nicholas said, his voice tense. "Something feels wrong."

From the shadows emerged a figure cloaked in dark robes. The figure's face was obscured, but their presence exuded a malevolent energy.

"Who are you?" Zhoha demanded, her voice trembling.

The cloaked figure's voice was cold and dispassionate. "I am the Guardian of the Heart. You were not meant to find it."

Nicholas and Zhoha braced themselves, realising that their quest was far from over. The Guardian's presence was a formidable obstacle, and they would need to face this challenge to uncover the full power of the Heart of the Elements.

The chamber seemed to close in around them as the Guardian stepped forward, the shadows growing darker and more oppressive. Nicholas and Zhoha prepared to confront the Guardian, determined to protect their hard-earned discovery and unlock the secrets of the hidden gem.

Their adventure was far from over, and the path ahead was fraught with danger and uncertainty. But with their resolve and the power of their artefacts, Nicholas and Zhoha were ready to face whatever lay ahead and uncover the full potential of the Heart of the Elements.

Chapter 6: The Trials

The chamber was thick with tension as the Guardian of the Heart of the Elements emerged from the shadows. Nicholas and Zhoha stood their ground, the weight of their discovery pressing heavily upon their shoulders. The Guardian's presence was both imposing and disquieting, casting an air of foreboding over the ancient chamber.

The Guardian's dark robes swirled with an almost supernatural grace as the figure moved forward, their voice echoing with a chilling authority. "You have ventured far and overcome many obstacles, but the final test awaits. The Heart of the Elements is not easily claimed. You must prove your worthiness through the trials of the Custodians."

Nicholas tightened his grip on the artefacts they had collected. "What are these trials? How can we prove ourselves worthy?"

The Guardian's obscured face revealed nothing, but a sense of anticipation seemed to emanate from the figure. "The trials are ancient tests designed to assess the virtues of those who seek the Heart. They are trials of courage, wisdom, and integrity. Only those who succeed in all three will be deemed worthy to claim the Heart."

The chamber was silent save for the distant hum of the crystal, its rhythmic pulse filling the space with an almost hypnotic energy. Nicholas and Zhoha exchanged determined glances. They had come too far to back down now.

"Where do we begin?" Zhoha asked, her voice steady despite the growing tension.

The Guardian gestured towards a hidden door that had begun to materialise in the far wall of the chamber. "The trials are hidden within this labyrinth. Each trial will test you in a different aspect. Complete them to gain access to the Heart. Fail, and you shall be forever bound to this place."

Without further ado, the Guardian vanished into the shadows, leaving Nicholas and Zhoha alone with the looming challenge ahead.

With a deep breath, they approached the newly revealed door, its surface covered in intricate runes and symbols similar to those they had encountered before.

The door creaked open, revealing a narrow, winding passageway. The walls were lined with ancient carvings, and the air grew colder as they stepped inside. The path ahead was shrouded in darkness, but the soft glow of the crystal provided a faint illumination.

"We need to stay focused," Nicholas said, adjusting the strap of his backpack. "These trials are meant to challenge us in ways we can't anticipate."

Zhoha nodded, her face set with resolve. "Let's proceed carefully. We've come this far, and we're not turning back now."

The passageway twisted and turned, and they soon reached the first trial. The chamber was illuminated by a flickering torchlight, casting eerie shadows on the walls. In the centre of the room stood a large pedestal with an inscription in an ancient script.

"This must be the trial of courage," Nicholas said, his voice echoing off the stone walls. "The inscription might give us clues on how to proceed."

Zhoha studied the inscription, her brow furrowed in concentration. "It's written in an old dialect, but I can make out some of the words. It speaks of facing one's fears and confronting the unknown."

As she translated the inscription, a sudden gust of wind swept through the chamber, extinguishing the torches and plunging them into darkness. The sound of footsteps echoed ominously, and the ground beneath them began to tremble.

"Stay close!" Nicholas called out, his voice strained. "We need to find the source of this disturbance."

In the darkness, they made out a series of shadowy figures emerging from the walls, their forms shifting and writhing as if alive. The figures seemed to be manifestations of their deepest fears, each one representing a different aspect of their anxieties.

Nicholas faced a towering shadow that embodied his fears of failure and inadequacy. He could feel the weight of his past mistakes pressing down on him. With a deep breath, he stepped forward, determined to confront the shadow and overcome his fear.

Zhoha faced a more personal fear—the shadow of her own insecurities and doubts. She had always struggled with feelings of self-doubt and uncertainty, but she knew she had to face these fears head-on.

Together, Nicholas and Zhoha fought through the darkness, their resolve strengthening with each step. The shadows seemed to recede as they confronted their fears, their courage shining through despite the overwhelming darkness.

As the last of the shadows dissipated, the torches reignited, bathing the chamber in a warm glow. The pedestal before them began to emit a soft light, revealing a hidden passageway.

"That was intense," Nicholas said, wiping the sweat from his brow. "But we made it through the trial of courage."

Zhoha nodded, her expression reflecting both relief and determination. "We've proven our courage. Let's see what the next trial has in store for us."

They proceeded through the hidden passageway and arrived at the second trial. This chamber was filled with ancient scrolls and books, and the air was thick with the scent of old parchment. In the centre of the room was a large, ornate book on a pedestal.

"This must be the trial of wisdom," Zhoha said, examining the room. "We need to solve a riddle or answer a question to proceed."

The book on the pedestal was open to a page with a complex riddle inscribed on it. Nicholas and Zhoha took turns reading and analysing the riddle, which spoke of the balance between knowledge and understanding.

After several minutes of intense concentration, they realised that the riddle was asking them to apply their knowledge to solve a practical problem. The answer required them to use clues from the surrounding scrolls and books.

With their combined knowledge and reasoning, Nicholas and Zhoha worked through the riddle, their minds working in tandem to uncover the solution. When they finally answered correctly, the pedestal glowed brightly, and a hidden door opened, leading to the final trial.

"This trial of wisdom was challenging," Nicholas said, as they entered the final chamber. "But we're almost there."

The final chamber was a serene, circular room with a single pedestal in the centre. The pedestal held a scale, with two empty pans suspended above it. On the wall was an inscription that read:

"To prove your integrity, you must balance the scales with what you value most. Only then will you reveal the path to the Heart."

Nicholas and Zhoha looked at each other, their expressions reflecting the weight of the final trial. They had to decide what they valued most and place it on the scales to balance them.

After a moment of contemplation, Nicholas placed the amulet they had discovered on one side of the scale, and Zhoha placed the dagger. Both items held significant meaning for them, representing their journey and their bond.

The scales balanced perfectly, and a soft light began to emanate from the pedestal. The inscription on the wall shifted to reveal a new passageway leading deeper into the labyrinth.

"We've done it," Zhoha said, her voice filled with awe. "We've completed the trials."

Nicholas nodded, his expression a mixture of exhaustion and triumph. "Let's see what lies beyond this passage."

They followed the newly revealed path, their steps echoing in the silence. The passage led them back to the central chamber where the

Heart of the Elements was housed. The chamber was now bathed in a brilliant light, and the Guardian's presence was gone.

The large chest on the pedestal remained open, and the glowing crystal within it seemed to pulse with a newfound intensity. Nicholas and Zhoha approached the chest, their hearts pounding with anticipation.

"This is it," Nicholas said, his voice trembling with excitement. "We've unlocked the Heart of the Elements."

As they reached for the crystal, a sense of profound energy surged through the chamber. The Heart of the Elements had been revealed in all its glory, and Nicholas and Zhoha knew that their journey had led them to the culmination of their quest.

With the trials behind them and the Heart within their grasp, they felt a deep sense of accomplishment and relief. The challenges they had faced had tested their courage, wisdom, and integrity, and they had emerged victorious.

"We did it," Zhoha said, her voice filled with pride. "We've achieved what we set out to do."

Nicholas smiled, his gaze fixed on the Heart of the Elements. "Yes, we did. And now, we must decide how to use this power wisely."

As they stood in the chamber, surrounded by the artefacts and the Heart of the Elements, they knew that their journey was far from over. The discovery of the Heart marked the beginning of a new chapter in their quest, one filled with the promise of new adventures and challenges.

With the Heart of the Elements in their possession and their resolve stronger than ever, Nicholas and Zhoha prepared to face the future, knowing that their journey had only just begun.

Chapter 7: Chained No More

The chamber, bathed in the ethereal glow of the Heart of the Elements, seemed to hum with newfound energy. Nicholas and Zhoha stood in reverent silence, their eyes fixed on the glowing crystal that now pulsed rhythmically before them. They had faced the trials, proven their worth, and obtained the Heart. But as they prepared to leave the chamber, a sense of unease began to settle over them.

The chamber's walls, adorned with intricate carvings depicting elemental forces, seemed to shimmer and shift in the crystal's light. The air crackled with a subtle electric charge, and the temperature fluctuated unpredictably, reflecting the Heart's potent energy.

"This is incredible," Nicholas said, his voice filled with awe as he carefully examined the Heart. "The power contained within this crystal is beyond anything I could have imagined."

Zhoha nodded, her eyes scanning the chamber with a mix of excitement and apprehension. "We need to be careful. We don't know the full extent of the Heart's power or its potential consequences."

As they prepared to leave the chamber, a sudden tremor shook the ground beneath them. The walls of the chamber seemed to pulse in response to the tremor, and a low rumbling noise reverberated through the labyrinth. The chamber's illumination flickered, casting eerie shadows that danced along the walls.

"What's happening?" Zhoha asked, her voice tinged with concern.

"I'm not sure," Nicholas replied, his gaze shifting to the pulsating Heart. "But it looks like the Heart's power might be affecting the entire labyrinth."

The rumbling intensified, and the chamber's entrance began to collapse, large stones falling from above and blocking the way they had come. Nicholas and Zhoha exchanged alarmed glances; they were trapped.

"We need to find another way out," Nicholas said urgently. "If the labyrinth is collapsing, we need to move quickly."

The glowing crystal seemed to respond to their urgency, its light growing brighter and more erratic. Nicholas and Zhoha navigated through the labyrinth, their path illuminated by the crystal's intense energy. The labyrinth's layout seemed to shift, walls moving and passages rearranging themselves as if the very structure was reacting to the Heart's power.

"Look!" Zhoha exclaimed, pointing to a newly revealed passageway. "That wasn't there before."

They hurried through the newly revealed path, the Heart's light guiding them through the maze-like corridors. As they progressed, the labyrinth's environment became increasingly unstable. The walls quaked, and the ground beneath them trembled. It was as if the labyrinth itself was resisting their escape.

"This is becoming dangerous," Nicholas said, his voice strained as he tried to keep his footing. "We need to find a way to stabilise the Heart's power or we might get trapped here."

They reached another chamber, larger and more ornate than the others they had encountered. In the centre of the chamber was a complex array of mechanisms and runes, seemingly designed to control or harness the Heart's energy. The chamber was filled with a faint, pulsing light that appeared to emanate from the mechanisms themselves.

"This looks like it might be a control room," Zhoha observed. "If we can figure out how to use these mechanisms, we might be able to stabilise the Heart's energy."

Nicholas and Zhoha approached the central mechanism, a large, intricate device with multiple levers and dials. The runes inscribed on the device matched some of the symbols they had seen throughout the labyrinth.

"We need to decipher these runes," Nicholas said, examining the device closely. "They might tell us how to control the Heart's energy."

Zhoha studied the runes and compared them with the inscriptions they had encountered earlier. "These symbols seem to be related to balancing forces—perhaps we need to adjust the mechanisms to create a balance."

With a sense of urgency, they began to manipulate the levers and dials according to their interpretation of the runes. The mechanisms whirred and clicked as they adjusted the settings, and the pulsing light from the Heart began to stabilise.

As the energy levels became more controlled, the chamber's tremors subsided, and the shifting walls of the labyrinth started to settle into place. The chaos that had engulfed the labyrinth seemed to be easing, and the pathway back to the central chamber became clearer.

"We did it," Zhoha said, her voice relieved. "The Heart's energy is stabilising."

Nicholas nodded, his expression a mix of exhaustion and relief. "Let's get back to the central chamber and see if we can find a way out."

They retraced their steps through the labyrinth, the paths now more stable and less chaotic. The central chamber was once again bathed in a steady, calming light. The entrance they had used to access the labyrinth was now clear, the rubble having been cleared away by the stabilisation of the Heart's power.

As they emerged from the labyrinth, the external world seemed to greet them with a sense of calm and serenity. The dense forest outside the entrance was bathed in the soft light of dawn, the trees swaying gently in the breeze.

"We made it out," Nicholas said, his voice filled with relief. "But we need to understand the implications of what we've discovered."

Zhoha nodded, her gaze fixed on the Heart of the Elements. "The Heart's power is immense. We need to be cautious about how we use it. There's no telling what might happen if it's misused."

They made their way back to their base of operations, carrying the Heart with great care. The journey back was quieter, the earlier sense of urgency replaced by contemplation. They had successfully retrieved the Heart, but the experience had left them with a deeper understanding of its power and the responsibilities that came with it.

Back at Zhoha's study, they carefully placed the Heart on a central pedestal. The glow of the crystal illuminated the room, casting a warm light on the manuscripts and artefacts that had guided their quest.

"We need to study this further," Nicholas said, taking a seat at the desk. "There might be additional information or warnings related to the Heart that we need to understand."

Zhoha nodded, her eyes scanning the manuscripts. "We also need to consider the potential consequences of wielding such power. There must be records or legends about how the Heart was used in the past."

As they delved into their research, the Heart's energy seemed to resonate with the ancient texts and symbols. The more they studied, the clearer it became that the Heart was not merely a source of power but also a conduit for elemental forces that could influence the world in profound ways.

Hours turned into days as Nicholas and Zhoha immersed themselves in their research. They discovered that the Heart had been a central element in ancient rituals and was believed to maintain balance among the elemental forces. It was clear that their responsibility was not just to possess the Heart but to ensure its power was used wisely and for the greater good.

One evening, as they pored over a particularly ancient manuscript, Zhoha's eyes widened. "Nicholas, look at this. It describes a ceremony for channelling the Heart's power to restore balance in times of great upheaval."

Nicholas leaned in, his interest piqued. "This could be crucial. If there's a ceremony for harnessing the Heart's power, it might help us understand how to use it responsibly."

Zhoha nodded, her expression determined. "We need to learn this ceremony and prepare ourselves for any potential challenges. The Heart's power is a great responsibility, and we must be prepared to face whatever comes next."

With their newfound knowledge and understanding, Nicholas and Zhoha felt a renewed sense of purpose. Their journey had led them to uncover the Heart of the Elements, but the true challenge now lay in wielding its power wisely and ensuring it was used to maintain balance and harmony in the world.

As they continued their research and preparation, they knew that their adventure was far from over. The Heart of the Elements had opened new paths and possibilities, and with it came a deeper understanding of the forces at play in their world.

Together, Nicholas and Zhoha embraced the challenge ahead, ready to face the responsibilities and adventures that awaited them. Their journey had only just begun, and the echoes of the Heart's power would guide them as they continued their quest for knowledge and balance.

Chapter 8: Call To Power

The morning sun filtered through the thick canopy of the ancient forest, casting dappled shadows on the path leading away from Zhoha's study. Nicholas and Zhoha, having spent several days immersed in their research, emerged from their sanctuary with a shared sense of purpose. They now had a clearer understanding of the Heart of the Elements and its potential, but the knowledge came with its own set of challenges.

The manuscript detailing the ancient ceremony had opened their eyes to the gravity of their task. It was clear that the Heart's power was not to be wielded lightly. The ceremony described was intended for times of great imbalance, suggesting that their discovery might be more critical than they initially thought. As they prepared to leave, their thoughts were interrupted by a distant rumble, a reminder that the power they now held could have far-reaching consequences.

"We need to visit the local sages and scholars," Nicholas said, adjusting the strap of his backpack. "There might be more information or even warnings about the Heart's effects on the world."

Zhoha nodded, her expression thoughtful. "Agreed. The balance of elemental forces is delicate. If the Heart's power has the potential to disrupt it, we must be prepared for any eventuality."

Their journey led them to a remote village nestled at the edge of the forest, where legends spoke of an ancient order known as the Guardians. These scholars and sages were rumoured to hold knowledge about the elemental forces and their historical significance. As they approached the village, a sense of anticipation mixed with trepidation settled over them.

The village elder, an old man with a long white beard and a piercing gaze, welcomed them with a mixture of curiosity and wariness. His name was Eldric, and he was known for his extensive knowledge of ancient lore.

"I have heard whispers of your quest," Eldric said, his voice gravelly with age. "You seek the Heart of the Elements. Few have ventured so far and lived to tell the tale."

Nicholas and Zhoha exchanged a look of mutual determination before Nicholas spoke. "We have indeed found the Heart. We need your guidance. Our research has revealed a ceremony for channelling its power, but we lack the full understanding of its implications and execution."

Eldric's eyes narrowed, and he motioned for them to follow him to a secluded area of the village, where an ancient library lay hidden. The library was filled with dusty tomes and scrolls, its air thick with the scent of aged parchment and ink.

"This library holds knowledge passed down through generations of Guardians," Eldric explained. "It may contain the information you seek."

Nicholas and Zhoha eagerly began to sift through the texts. They discovered references to the Heart of the Elements scattered among various volumes. Some texts spoke of the Heart's role in maintaining harmony among the elemental forces, while others hinted at its potential to cause great upheaval if misused.

One particularly ancient scroll detailed a prophecy that spoke of a time when the Heart would be needed to restore balance to a world on the brink of chaos. The prophecy mentioned an "Echo of Power," a sign that the Heart's influence was needed to counteract a looming threat.

"This prophecy could be related to the recent disturbances," Zhoha said, her eyes scanning the text. "It seems to suggest that the Heart's power could either save or doom the world, depending on how it's used."

Nicholas nodded, his expression grave. "We need to understand this 'Echo of Power.' If there's a looming threat, we must be prepared to face it."

Eldric, who had been quietly observing their progress, stepped forward. "The Echo of Power is a phenomenon that occurs when the elemental forces are thrown out of balance. It is a call for intervention from the Guardians to restore equilibrium."

Nicholas and Zhoha listened intently as Eldric continued. "The prophecy speaks of a convergence of elemental forces, a time when the Heart's power will be tested. If you've already felt the effects of the Heart's power, it is possible that the Echo has begun."

As they absorbed Eldric's words, a sense of urgency gripped them. The implications of the prophecy suggested that their quest was far from over. They needed to prepare for a larger conflict that could threaten the very fabric of their world.

"Is there any way to mitigate the effects of the Echo or prevent it from escalating?" Zhoha asked, her voice filled with concern.

Eldric nodded, his face thoughtful. "There are rituals and artefacts that can help stabilise the elemental forces. But they require great knowledge and skill to perform. The Guardians have safeguarded such rituals for centuries, but they must be undertaken with caution."

Nicholas and Zhoha understood the gravity of their task. They needed to seek out these rituals and artefacts and gain further understanding of how to use the Heart responsibly. They spent the next few days in the village, learning from Eldric and other scholars about the rituals and practices necessary to control the Heart's power.

With newfound knowledge and a sense of purpose, Nicholas and Zhoha set out on their journey once more. They travelled to various locations mentioned in the ancient texts, seeking out artefacts and gathering information. Their journey took them through ancient ruins, hidden temples, and sacred groves, each location revealing more about the elemental forces and their intricate balance.

At each stop, they encountered challenges that tested their resolve. They deciphered ancient puzzles, navigated treacherous terrain, and confronted elemental guardians who tested their worthiness. Each challenge brought them closer to understanding the Heart's power and how to wield it.

One evening, as they rested by a tranquil lake, Zhoha reflected on their journey. "We've learned so much, but it feels like we're only scratching the surface. The more we uncover, the more complex this quest becomes."

Nicholas nodded, his gaze fixed on the lake's shimmering surface. "The Heart of the Elements is a conduit for immense power. Our responsibility is not just to wield it but to understand it deeply. The balance we seek to maintain is delicate and crucial."

As they continued their quest, Nicholas and Zhoha grew more confident in their ability to handle the Heart's power. They had learned to channel its energy in ways that supported the elemental forces rather than disrupt them. Their bond as a team grew stronger, forged through their shared experiences and challenges.

One night, while camped beneath a starlit sky, they received a vision in their dreams. The vision was a vivid portrayal of the convergence of elemental forces described in the prophecy. It showed a great upheaval, with the Heart's power playing a central role in restoring balance.

Nicholas awoke with a start, his heart pounding. "Zhoha, I had a vision. It showed the convergence of the elemental forces and the Heart's role in restoring balance."

Zhoha stirred, her eyes wide with concern. "We need to be prepared for whatever is coming. The vision might be a sign that the Echo of Power is imminent."

With renewed determination, Nicholas and Zhoha pressed on with their preparations. They completed the rituals and gathered the necessary artefacts, readying themselves for the challenges ahead. Their journey had prepared them for the critical moment when the Heart's power would be needed most.

As they approached the final stages of their quest, the sense of impending change grew stronger. The balance of elemental forces hung in the balance, and Nicholas and Zhoha knew that their actions would have a profound impact on the world.

They reached the heart of the disturbance, a place where the elemental forces were most chaotic. The landscape was marked by swirling storms, shifting earth, and flickering flames. The convergence of the elements was at its peak, and the Heart's power was needed to restore balance.

Nicholas and Zhoha took their positions, ready to perform the ancient rituals they had learned. The Heart of the Elements glowed brightly, its energy resonating with the surrounding chaos. With focused intent, they began the ceremony, channelling the Heart's power to stabilise the elemental forces.

The process was intense and demanding, requiring precise coordination and unwavering focus. The Heart's energy surged and flowed, interacting with the elements to restore harmony. As the ritual progressed, the chaotic forces began to settle, and the landscape started to stabilise.

After hours of effort, the balance was restored. The swirling storms abated, the earth settled, and the flames flickered gently. The elemental forces were once again in harmony, and the Heart's power had achieved its intended purpose.

Nicholas and Zhoha, exhausted but triumphant, stood amidst the restored landscape. The journey had been arduous, but they had succeeded in their mission. The Heart of the Elements had proven its worth, and they had fulfilled their role as its guardians.

As they made their way back to the village, they knew that their adventure had come full circle. The balance of the elemental forces had been restored, and the Heart's power had been used wisely. Their journey had not only tested their abilities but had also deepened their understanding of the world's intricate balance.

Nicholas and Zhoha returned to their base of operations with a sense of fulfilment and a renewed commitment to their role as custodians of the Heart. Their journey had forged a bond between them and had prepared them for any future challenges that might arise.

With the Heart of the Elements now stabilised and the balance restored, they looked forward to the future with hope and determination. Their quest had been a profound journey of discovery and responsibility, and they were ready to face whatever lay ahead.

The echoes of the Heart's power would continue to guide them, and their adventure was far from over. The world was full of mysteries and challenges, and Nicholas and Zhoha were prepared to meet them with courage and wisdom.

Chapter 9: Fractured Peace

The morning after their successful restoration of balance, Nicholas and Zhoha awoke to a sky tinged with a golden hue, signalling the start of a new day. The forest surrounding their temporary camp was quiet, save for the gentle rustling of leaves and the distant calls of birds. Despite the tranquillity of the scene, both of them knew that their journey was far from over.

Nicholas stretched, the weariness of the previous night's efforts still evident in his movements. "It's strange," he said, gazing at the peaceful landscape. "After everything we've been through, it feels almost surreal to see the world so calm."

Zhoha, who was meticulously packing their belongings, glanced up. "The calm before the storm, perhaps. The Echo of Power might have been quelled for now, but we must remain vigilant. The Heart's influence is still a concern."

As they prepared to leave, a messenger from the village arrived, bearing urgent news. The messenger, a young woman with an anxious expression, relayed a troubling report: a nearby town was experiencing unexplained disturbances—severe weather anomalies, erratic magical surges, and unusual creature behaviour. The villagers were growing desperate and had called for the Guardians' aid.

"This sounds like the work of lingering effects from the imbalance," Zhoha said, her brow furrowed with concern. "We need to investigate."

Nicholas nodded, and they quickly gathered their things. The journey to the affected town was brisk, their urgency matched by the increasing signs of trouble as they approached. Dark clouds loomed overhead, and the once-familiar landscape now bore the marks of chaotic elemental disturbances.

When they arrived, they were met by the town's mayor, an elderly woman named Mara. Her face was etched with worry as she described the situation. "We've never seen anything like this," she said, gesturing to the tumultuous skies above. "The storms have grown violent, and strange creatures have been spotted near the outskirts. We fear for our safety."

Nicholas and Zhoha took in the scene. The sky was a roiling mass of dark clouds, lightning crackling erratically. The once-serene town was now in disarray, with people running for shelter and trying to protect their homes.

"We'll do what we can to help," Nicholas assured Mara. "We need to understand the source of these disturbances."

As they began their investigation, they noticed that the elemental disturbances seemed localised around a specific area on the town's outskirts. A series of ancient runes, half-buried and partially hidden by overgrowth, caught their attention. The runes were faint but recognizable as being linked to the Heart's elemental forces.

"This could be related to the Echo of Power," Zhoha suggested. "If these runes are tied to the disturbances, we might be able to reverse the effects by understanding their purpose."

They carefully began to examine and decipher the runes, which appeared to be part of a larger, more complex array. The runes were inscribed in a circle, each one representing a different elemental force. As they worked, the disturbances around them seemed to intensify, with sudden gusts of wind and erratic bursts of energy.

Nicholas and Zhoha realised that the runes were malfunctioning, likely due to the disruption caused by the Heart's previous imbalance. If the runes were not restored or corrected, the disturbances could worsen.

"We need to stabilise these runes," Nicholas said, his voice raised over the howling wind. "But we must proceed carefully. Disrupting them further could have unpredictable consequences."

Zhoha nodded and began to adjust the runes, using her knowledge of the Heart's energy to realign them. Nicholas assisted by providing support and ensuring that the runes' energies were properly channelled.

As they worked, they felt the Heart's influence guiding them, helping to restore balance to the elemental forces.

The process was delicate and demanded precise control. Every adjustment to the runes seemed to affect the surrounding environment, with the storms and disturbances gradually beginning to subside as they worked.

After hours of intense effort, the runes were realigned, and the chaotic elemental forces began to stabilise. The storm clouds started to dissipate, and the erratic bursts of energy ceased. The town slowly returned to a semblance of normalcy, though the damage was evident.

Mara approached them with a look of relief. "Thank you for your help. The disturbances have eased, and we can begin to repair the damage."

Nicholas and Zhoha exchanged a look of mutual satisfaction. "We're glad we could help," Nicholas said. "But we need to investigate further. These disturbances might be a sign of a deeper issue."

As they prepared to leave the town, Eldric's words from their previous visit echoed in their minds. The convergence of elemental forces was not a solitary event; it was part of a larger pattern that required ongoing vigilance.

Their next step was to seek out additional information about the runes and their purpose. They travelled to ancient libraries and consulted with scholars who specialised in elemental magic and ancient rituals. Their research revealed that the runes were part of a larger network of elemental conduits, designed to maintain balance and channel elemental forces.

The deeper they delved, the more they learned about the interconnected nature of the elemental forces. The Heart of the Elements was a key component, but it was clear that other artefacts and rituals were also essential for maintaining balance. The runes they had encountered were merely one part of a larger system.

One evening, while studying an old manuscript in a secluded library, Zhoha came across a reference to a hidden repository of knowledge related to the elemental forces. According to the manuscript, this repository contained ancient texts and artefacts that could provide further insight into the disturbances and the Echo of Power.

"This repository could hold the answers we need," Zhoha said, her eyes alight with excitement. "We should find it and explore its contents."

Nicholas agreed, and they set out on a new quest to locate the hidden repository. Their journey took them through treacherous terrain, including dense forests, towering mountains, and winding caves. Along the way, they faced various challenges, including natural hazards and elemental creatures guarding the repository's entrance.

After several days of arduous travel, they finally reached the repository's location—an ancient, hidden cavern deep within a mountain range. The cavern was adorned with intricate carvings and symbols that hinted at its importance.

Inside the cavern, they discovered a wealth of ancient texts, artefacts, and relics related to the elemental forces. The repository's contents were organised meticulously, and it was clear that it had been safeguarded for centuries by the Guardians.

Nicholas and Zhoha spent hours exploring the repository, uncovering valuable information about the elemental forces and their interactions. They learned about additional rituals and artefacts that could help stabilise the balance and counteract the Echo of Power.

One artefact in particular—a crystal shard imbued with elemental energy—caught their attention. The shard appeared to be a key component in performing advanced rituals to maintain balance among the elemental forces.

"This artefact could be crucial for our next steps," Nicholas said, examining the shard closely. "We need to understand its properties and how to use it effectively."

Zhoha nodded, her expression determined. "With this artefact and the knowledge we've gained, we should be better prepared to handle any future disturbances."

As they left the repository, Nicholas and Zhoha felt a renewed sense of purpose. Their quest was far from over, but they were now better equipped to address the challenges ahead. The Heart of the Elements, the ancient runes, and the newly discovered artefact were all interconnected, and they needed to ensure that the balance among the elemental forces was maintained.

Back in the village, they continued their efforts to repair the damage caused by the recent disturbances. They worked closely with the villagers, helping to restore their homes and infrastructure. The town's recovery was slow but steady, and the people were grateful for the Guardians' assistance.

Nicholas and Zhoha knew that their role was far from finished. The elemental forces were complex and ever-changing, and their responsibility was to ensure that balance was maintained. With the knowledge and artefacts they had acquired, they were prepared to face whatever challenges lay ahead.

As they looked out over the recovering town, Nicholas and Zhoha felt a sense of accomplishment and hope. Their journey had brought them closer to understanding the intricate balance of the elemental forces, and they were ready to continue their quest to protect and preserve that balance.

Their adventure was a testament to their dedication and courage, and they knew that their efforts would have a lasting impact on the world. With the Heart of the Elements and their newfound knowledge, Nicholas and Zhoha were poised to face the future with confidence and resolve. The echoes of their journey would guide them as they continued to navigate the complexities of the elemental forces and uphold the balance that sustained their world.

Chapter 10: Dark Side

The dawn broke with a crisp, clear light as Nicholas and Zhoha made their way from the recovering town. The journey ahead was uncertain, but the knowledge and artefacts they had gathered bolstered their resolve. Their recent successes had reaffirmed their commitment to their mission, but they knew that deeper challenges awaited them.

"We need to decide our next move," Nicholas said, breaking the silence that had settled between them as they walked. "The disturbances we've seen could be just the beginning."

Zhoha nodded, her eyes scanning the landscape for any signs of trouble. "The repository provided valuable insights, but it also hinted at a larger threat. We must find out more about the origins of the Heart and its connection to these disturbances."

As they travelled, they discussed their findings from the repository. The crystal shard they had discovered was indeed a powerful artefact, capable of amplifying and directing elemental energies. However, it was clear that it's true potential—and its limits—could only be understood by uncovering more about the Heart's history and purpose.

Their journey led them to a distant city known for its ancient archives and scholars specialising in arcane history. The city, surrounded by imposing walls and bustling with activity, was a stark contrast to the serene landscapes they had traversed.

Upon arrival, they were greeted by a local scholar named Elara, who was renowned for her knowledge of ancient artefacts and magical history. Elara welcomed them into her study, a grand chamber filled with scrolls, tomes, and mystical artefacts.

"You've come at a fortuitous time," Elara said as she led them to a table laden with ancient texts. "I've recently uncovered references to an old legend that might be related to the disturbances you've described."

Nicholas and Zhoha listened intently as Elara explained the legend. It spoke of an ancient conflict between elemental forces that had once threatened to tear the world apart. The legend described a powerful entity—an elemental being of immense strength—that had been sealed away by the Guardians to prevent its destructive influence from resurfacing.

"This entity, known as the Voidbringer, was said to be a force of pure chaos," Elara said, her voice tinged with awe. "The legend suggests that the Heart of the Elements was created to counterbalance the Voidbringer's influence and maintain equilibrium among the elemental forces."

Zhoha's eyes widened. "If the Voidbringer is connected to the current disturbances, then the Heart's recent imbalance could have inadvertently awakened it or weakened its seal."

Elara nodded. "It's a possibility. The legend also speaks of a hidden chamber, deep within the elemental realm, where the Voidbringer's seal is maintained. The chamber is guarded by ancient wards and protected by powerful elemental beings."

Nicholas and Zhoha exchanged a determined glance. "We need to find this hidden chamber and ensure that the Voidbringer's seal remains intact," Nicholas said. "If it's been weakened, the consequences could be catastrophic."

Elara agreed to assist them in their quest by providing access to her archives and any additional knowledge she could offer. For several days, Nicholas and Zhoha pored over ancient texts and consulted with Elara. They discovered that the location of the hidden chamber was linked to a series of elemental alignments and clues scattered throughout the world.

Their research pointed them toward a remote region known for its elemental anomalies and ancient ruins. The region, characterised by its rugged terrain and unpredictable weather, was rumoured to be a place of great mystical significance.

As they set out for the region, Nicholas and Zhoha encountered a series of trials that tested their skills and knowledge. The elemental anomalies in the area created a challenging environment, with sudden storms, shifting landscapes, and erratic magical surges.

Despite these challenges, they pressed on, guided by their determination and the clues they had gathered. The journey led them to an ancient ruin partially buried beneath the shifting sands of a desert. The ruin's entrance was marked by intricate carvings that matched the symbols they had seen in Elara's texts.

Inside the ruin, they navigated a series of chambers, each representing a different elemental force. The chambers were filled with puzzles and traps designed to test their understanding of the elements and their ability to maintain balance.

The final chamber, hidden behind a heavy stone door, was decorated with symbols representing the Voidbringer's seal. Nicholas and Zhoha carefully examined the symbols, deciphering the ancient wards that protected the chamber.

"This must be it," Zhoha said, her voice echoing in the chamber. "The seal is intact, but it looks like it's been weakened."

Nicholas examined the symbols more closely. "We need to reinforce the seal and restore its strength. The Voidbringer's influence could have far-reaching consequences if it's allowed to break free."

Using the knowledge and artefacts they had acquired, Nicholas and Zhoha performed a ritual to reinforce the seal. The process was intricate and required precise coordination, but their combined skills and determination ensured that the ritual was successful.

As they completed the ritual, the chamber's atmosphere shifted, and a sense of calm settled over them. The Voidbringer's seal was once again reinforced, and the elemental forces seemed to stabilise.

With their task accomplished, Nicholas and Zhoha began their journey back to the city. Their path was marked by a newfound sense of accomplishment and relief, but they knew that their responsibilities were far from over.

Back in the city, they met with Elara to report on their findings. Elara was impressed by their success and expressed her gratitude for their efforts. "Your work has restored balance and prevented a great threat from emerging," she said. "The knowledge you've gained will be invaluable for future generations of scholars and Guardians."

Nicholas and Zhoha thanked Elara for her assistance and support. They had learned much about the interconnected nature of the elemental forces and the importance of maintaining balance. The Heart of the Elements, the Voidbringer's seal, and the various artefacts they had encountered were all integral to preserving harmony in the world.

As they prepared to leave the city, Nicholas and Zhoha reflected on their journey. They had faced numerous challenges and uncovered profound truths about the elemental forces. Their quest had brought them closer to understanding their role as Guardians and the responsibilities that came with it.

"We've come a long way," Nicholas said as they stood at the city's edge, looking out over the horizon. "But there's still much to learn and more challenges to face."

Zhoha nodded. "The balance of the elemental forces is delicate, and our role is crucial. We must remain vigilant and continue to protect the harmony of the world."

With their resolve strengthened, Nicholas and Zhoha set out on their next adventure, ready to confront whatever challenges lay ahead. The echoes of their journey had guided them to this point, and they were prepared to face the future with courage and wisdom.

Their path was uncertain, but their dedication to their mission was unwavering. The Heart of the Elements, the Voidbringer's seal, and the lessons they had learned would continue to shape their journey. As they ventured forth, Nicholas and Zhoha were ready to uphold the balance of the elemental forces and ensure the world's continued harmony.

Their adventure was far from over, and they knew that their efforts would have a lasting impact on the world. With each step they took, they moved closer to their ultimate goal—to protect and preserve the delicate balance that sustained their world and to face whatever challenges the future might hold.

Chapter 11: The Hidden Gem

The journey from the city to their next destination was filled with a mix of excitement and unease. Nicholas and Zhoha had gathered significant knowledge and artefacts, but the weight of their responsibilities was heavy. As they travelled, they discussed their next steps, which involved exploring ancient legends and uncovering further secrets about the Heart of the Elements.

"I keep thinking about that crystal shard," Zhoha said as they walked along a winding path through a dense forest. "Elara mentioned it could be crucial for our next steps, but we don't fully understand its potential."

Nicholas nodded, his brow furrowed in thought. "We need to determine how to harness its power effectively. It might be the key to stabilising the Heart or counteracting any future disturbances."

Their path led them to a secluded mountain range, rumoured to be home to an ancient, hidden temple. According to their research, the temple was a place of great significance, linked to the elemental forces and potentially containing more information about the crystal shard.

As they approached the base of the mountains, the landscape began to change. The forest gave way to rocky terrain, and the air grew cooler. They followed a narrow trail that snaked up the mountainside, their progress slow due to the challenging terrain.

After several hours of climbing, they reached a plateau where the remains of the ancient temple came into view. The temple's grand entrance was partially obscured by overgrowth, but its intricate carvings and majestic pillars still bore witness to its former glory.

"This must be it," Nicholas said, his voice filled with awe as he took in the sight. "Let's see if we can find a way inside."

The entrance was guarded by a massive stone door adorned with ancient symbols similar to those they had seen in the Voidbringer's chamber. Zhoha approached the door and began to study the symbols.

"These symbols seem to represent different elemental forces," she said. "They might be part of a mechanism to open the door. We'll need to align them in the correct order."

As they worked on deciphering the symbols, a sudden gust of wind swept through the area, and the temperature dropped. The elements seemed to react to their presence, and the door's carvings began to glow faintly.

"This might be a test," Nicholas speculated. "The temple could be protecting something valuable."

With careful coordination, Nicholas and Zhoha aligned the symbols based on their knowledge of elemental balance. As they completed the arrangement, the stone door creaked open, revealing a dimly lit corridor leading into the heart of the temple.

They entered the corridor, their footsteps echoing off the ancient stone walls. The air was thick with the scent of old parchment and incense. The corridor led them to a large chamber filled with relics and artefacts related to the elemental forces.

In the centre of the chamber stood a pedestal with a glowing crystal—a perfect match for the shard they had discovered earlier. The pedestal was surrounded by an elaborate array of runes, and the crystal's light seemed to pulse in rhythm with their own heartbeats.

"This is incredible," Zhoha said, her eyes wide with wonder. "It's as if the crystal was meant to be here."

Nicholas approached the pedestal cautiously. "We should be careful. There might be additional wards or traps designed to protect this chamber."

As he reached out to examine the crystal, a sudden, low rumble echoed through the chamber. The ground beneath them shifted slightly, and a series of elemental guardians—ethereal beings representing the core forces of earth, water, fire, and air—emerged from the shadows.

The guardians observed Nicholas and Zhoha with a mixture of curiosity and vigilance. They seemed to be waiting for an indication of whether the intruders were friend or foe.

"We come in peace," Nicholas said, holding up his hands in a gesture of respect. "We seek to understand and protect the balance of the elemental forces. We believe this crystal holds the key to our mission."

One of the guardians, an ethereal figure of swirling water, spoke in a voice that resonated like a distant storm. "To seek the crystal is to seek the truth of the elements. Prove your worth, and you may take what you seek."

Zhoha stepped forward, her voice steady. "We are Guardians dedicated to maintaining balance. We have already faced many trials to protect the world from chaos."

The elemental guardians exchanged glances, and the air grew charged with energy. The water guardian extended a hand, and a series of challenges materialised before Nicholas and Zhoha. Each challenge tested their understanding of the elemental forces and their ability to maintain harmony.

The first challenge involved manipulating fire to ignite a series of torches without allowing any of them to go out. The second required them to channel water to flow through intricate channels, ensuring that every path was filled without overflow. The third tested their ability to control the wind to move objects into precise positions, and the fourth demanded that they balance earth to form a stable structure.

Nicholas and Zhoha worked together, using their knowledge and skills to overcome each challenge. Their efforts were guided by the understanding they had gained from their previous experiences and the wisdom imparted by the ancient texts.

As they completed the final challenge, the elemental guardians nodded in approval. The crystal on the pedestal glowed brightly, and the runes around it began to shift and change, revealing a hidden compartment.

Inside the compartment lay an ancient scroll, bound in a material that seemed to shimmer with elemental energy. Zhoha carefully unrolled the scroll, revealing intricate diagrams and text detailing advanced rituals for harnessing the crystal's power and stabilising the elemental forces.

"This scroll contains knowledge about the crystal and its use in maintaining balance," Zhoha said, her voice filled with excitement. "It explains how to harness its power to enhance and stabilise elemental energies."

Nicholas examined the scroll closely. "This will be invaluable for our mission. We need to study these rituals and understand how to apply them."

As they prepared to leave the temple, the elemental guardians approached them once more. The water guardian spoke with a tone of respect. "You have proven your worth and demonstrated your commitment to balance. Use the crystal wisely and protect the harmony of the elements."

Nicholas and Zhoha thanked the guardians and made their way out of the temple. The crystal and scroll were carefully packed, their significance clear. They knew that their journey was far from over and that the knowledge they had gained would be crucial for their next steps.

Their return to the city was marked by a renewed sense of purpose. Nicholas and Zhoha were eager to delve deeper into the rituals outlined in the scroll and integrate the crystal's power into their efforts to maintain balance.

Back in their quarters, they spent days studying the scroll and practising the rituals. The knowledge they had acquired provided new insights into the elemental forces and the ways in which they could be harnessed and balanced.

The rituals required precision and focus, but Nicholas and Zhoha were determined to master them. They knew that their success in applying these rituals would be crucial for addressing future disturbances and ensuring the stability of the elemental forces.

As they worked, they reflected on their journey and the challenges they had faced. The discovery of the hidden temple and the knowledge contained in the scroll had brought them closer to their goal, but they were aware that there were still many unknowns and potential threats.

"We've made great progress," Nicholas said, looking over the scroll's diagrams. "But we need to remain vigilant. There's always the possibility of new disturbances or hidden threats."

Zhoha agreed. "The balance of the elemental forces is delicate, and our role as Guardians is more important than ever. We must be prepared for whatever challenges come our way."

With their newfound knowledge and the power of the crystal, Nicholas and Zhoha felt more equipped to handle the trials ahead. Their commitment to their mission was unwavering, and they were ready to face whatever the future held.

As they looked out over the city, they knew that their journey was far from complete. The elemental forces were vast and complex, and their role as Guardians required constant vigilance and dedication.

With a sense of determination and hope, Nicholas and Zhoha set their sights on the horizon, ready to continue their quest to protect and preserve the balance of the world. The echoes of their past adventures guided them, and they were prepared to face the challenges of the future with courage and resolve.

Their path lay ahead, filled with unknowns and possibilities. But with the knowledge they had gained and the strength of their purpose, Nicholas and Zhoha were ready to confront whatever awaited them and uphold the harmony of the elemental forces.

Chapter 12: The Resonance of Echoes

The city's skyline shimmered in the morning light, casting long shadows across the bustling streets below. Nicholas and Zhoha stood atop the city walls, overlooking the horizon with a renewed sense of purpose. The ancient scroll and the crystal shard they had recovered were powerful tools, but they understood that their mission required more than just knowledge and artefacts. It demanded an understanding of how to use these elements to maintain balance.

"What's next?" Zhoha asked, her gaze fixed on the distant landscape. "We've learned a great deal, but the world is vast and filled with unknowns."

Nicholas adjusted the strap of his pack and pulled out the scroll, spreading it across a nearby table. The diagrams and rituals detailed on its surface were intricate and complex, yet they held the key to harnessing the crystal's power effectively.

"I believe we need to seek out the elemental ley lines," Nicholas said. "These are the currents of elemental energy that flow through the world. They're mentioned in the scroll as vital channels for stabilising or amplifying elemental forces."

Zhoha nodded. "Ley lines could indeed be crucial. They connect various sites of elemental significance and might be the key to understanding how to use the crystal effectively."

The first ley line they sought was rumoured to converge at a site known as the Elemental Nexus, an ancient shrine said to be a focal point of the world's elemental energies. The Nexus was located in a remote region, surrounded by dense forests and rugged terrain, far from the familiar confines of the city.

Their journey to the Nexus was arduous. The terrain became increasingly challenging as they travelled deeper into the forest, with narrow paths and steep inclines. The air grew thick with the scent of earth and foliage, and the sounds of wildlife were a constant backdrop to their trek.

After several days of travel, they arrived at the base of a steep hill covered in ancient trees. At the top of the hill, partially hidden by the dense canopy, lay the entrance to the Elemental Nexus. The entrance was marked by weathered stone pillars, covered in moss and entwined with vines.

"This must be it," Nicholas said, his voice filled with anticipation. "Let's see if we can find a way inside."

They approached the entrance, carefully clearing away the overgrowth that obscured the doorway. As they worked, Zhoha noticed faint symbols carved into the stone. These symbols matched those they had seen in the hidden temple, suggesting a connection between the two sites.

"The symbols here are similar to those we encountered before," Zhoha remarked. "They might be part of a larger system of protection or guidance."

With their knowledge of elemental symbols and mechanisms, Nicholas and Zhoha managed to unlock the entrance, revealing a dark passageway leading into the heart of the Nexus. They lit their torches and ventured inside, their steps echoing in the confined space.

The interior of the Nexus was an expansive chamber, illuminated by a soft, ethereal light that seemed to emanate from the walls themselves. The chamber was filled with intricate carvings and statues representing the four elements—earth, water, fire, and air. In the centre of the chamber stood an ancient altar, upon which rested a large crystal, pulsating with a rhythmic glow.

"This altar must be where the ley lines converge," Nicholas said, his voice reverberating in the chamber. "The crystal here appears to be a focal point for the elemental energies."

Zhoha examined the altar closely. "We need to perform a ritual to align the crystal with the ley lines. According to the scroll, the ritual involves channelling the elemental energies through the crystal to stabilise the surrounding forces."

Nicholas nodded. "Let's set up the ritual. We'll need to harness each element in its appropriate form and direct it through the crystal."

They gathered the necessary materials from their packs—earth from the forest floor, water from a nearby stream, fire from a portable flame, and air from the ambient atmosphere. With the elements in place, they began the ritual, carefully following the instructions outlined in the scroll.

The ritual required precise coordination. Nicholas and Zhoha worked in harmony, channelling each element through the crystal while reciting the ancient incantations. The process was intense, and the chamber's atmosphere grew charged with energy. The crystal's glow intensified, casting vibrant patterns of light across the walls.

As they completed the ritual, the chamber was filled with a harmonious resonance—a deep, resonant hum that seemed to connect with the very fabric of the world. The crystal's glow settled into a steady, calming light, and the elemental energies surrounding the Nexus appeared to stabilise.

"Is it working?" Zhoha asked, her voice tinged with both exhaustion and hope.

Nicholas checked the readings from the elemental sensors they had brought along. "Yes, the energies are aligning. The ley lines are stabilising, and the Nexus is resonating with the crystal's energy."

With the ritual complete, they took a moment to rest and reflect. The Nexus, once a site of latent power, now seemed to be at peace, its energies balanced and harmonised. Nicholas and Zhoha understood that their work was making a tangible impact on the world's elemental forces.

"Next, we need to investigate the other ley lines," Nicholas said, looking over the scroll. "There are several more sites mentioned, each with its own significance."

Zhoha nodded. "We should continue our journey and ensure that all the lines are aligned. The balance of the elemental forces is delicate, and our efforts will help maintain it."

Their next destination was an ancient forest known for its mysterious energy anomalies. The forest was said to be another key point along the ley lines, and the scroll indicated that it held important clues for further stabilising the elemental forces.

The forest was dense and foreboding, with twisted trees and tangled underbrush creating a labyrinthine landscape. As they ventured deeper into the woods, they encountered various magical creatures and strange phenomena, each indicative of the forest's potent energies.

Despite the challenges, Nicholas and Zhoha pressed on, guided by their determination and the knowledge they had gained. They navigated the forest's twists and turns, using their understanding of elemental magic to overcome obstacles and decipher clues.

After several days of exploration, they arrived at a secluded glade where the energies of the forest converged. In the centre of the glade was an ancient stone circle, covered in runes and symbols related to the elements.

"This must be the site we're looking for," Zhoha said, examining the stone circle. "The runes here correspond to those in the scroll."

They set up their equipment and prepared to perform another ritual, this time to align the energies of the forest with the ley lines. The process was similar to their previous work, involving the channelling of elemental forces through the central stone circle.

As they completed the ritual, the forest's energy seemed to settle into a harmonious balance. The anomalies that had previously disturbed the area were resolved, and the magical creatures that had been restless became calm and serene.

With their task accomplished, Nicholas and Zhoha took a moment to appreciate the peaceful surroundings. The forest, once a place of uncertainty and imbalance, now seemed to be at ease, its energies aligned with the ley lines.

Their journey continued, with each ley line they encountered bringing new challenges and discoveries. The knowledge they gained from the scroll and their experiences in the field helped them navigate these challenges and make significant progress in their mission.

As they travelled from one site to the next, Nicholas and Zhoha reflected on their journey and the lessons they had learned. They had faced numerous trials, uncovered ancient secrets, and made a tangible impact on the balance of the elemental forces.

"We've come a long way," Nicholas said, looking back at the path they had travelled. "But there's still much more to do."

Zhoha agreed. "The balance of the elements is delicate, and our work is far from over. We must remain vigilant and continue to protect the harmony of the world."

With a renewed sense of purpose, Nicholas and Zhoha set out for their next destination. The journey ahead was filled with unknowns, but they were ready to face whatever challenges lay ahead. Their commitment to their mission and their dedication to preserving the balance of the elemental forces guided them as they continued their quest.

Their path was filled with potential and promise, and each step brought them closer to their ultimate goal. With the knowledge they had gained and the strength of their resolve, Nicholas and Zhoha were prepared to confront the future with courage and determination.

As they looked out over the horizon, the world seemed to hold its breath, awaiting their next move. With each challenge they overcame, they moved closer to fulfilling their role as Guardians and ensuring the continued harmony of the elemental forces. The journey was far from over, but with their unwavering dedication, Nicholas and Zhoha were ready to face whatever lay ahead.

Chapter 13: The Whispering Shadows

The following morning, Nicholas and Zhoha prepared for their next leg of the journey. The air was crisp, and the early light filtered through the window of their quarters, casting a warm glow over their plans. They had decided to travel to a site known as the Shadowed Vale, a place steeped in legend and said to hold ancient secrets linked to the elemental ley lines.

According to the scroll, the Shadowed Vale was a place where the balance of the elemental forces could be subtly influenced by the presence of ancient artefacts buried within the vale. The site was reputed to be protected by ancient wards, and it was crucial for Nicholas and Zhoha to approach with caution.

"Are we ready?" Zhoha asked, glancing at Nicholas as he packed the last of their supplies.

Nicholas nodded, his expression serious. "We need to be thorough in our preparations. The Shadowed Vale has a reputation for being unpredictable, and the artefacts we seek could be guarded by more than just natural barriers."

With their gear packed and their minds focused, they set out towards the vale. The journey took them through diverse landscapes, from rolling hills to deep, mist-covered valleys. As they neared the vale, the forest became denser, and the atmosphere grew heavier with an almost palpable sense of ancient power.

The entrance to the vale was marked by towering stone pillars covered in dark, twisting vines. The air was thick with an almost tangible energy, and the shadows seemed to dance unnaturally among the trees.

"This place feels different," Nicholas said, his voice low. "There's an underlying energy here that's hard to pinpoint."

Zhoha took a deep breath, her senses attuned to the subtle shifts in the environment. "We should proceed with caution. The scroll mentioned that the vale is protected by illusions and deceptive magic."

As they entered the vale, the environment shifted subtly. The once-familiar path seemed to twist and turn in unpredictable ways. Shadows flickered at the edges of their vision, and the trees seemed to whisper softly.

"Stay close," Nicholas instructed, his hand resting on the hilt of his blade. "We don't know what kinds of protections or guardians might be here."

The vale's heart was a cavernous grotto, filled with ancient stone formations and faintly glowing runes. The air was cool and damp, and the walls of the grotto were covered in a network of intricate patterns that pulsed faintly with energy.

"This must be where the artefacts are hidden," Zhoha said, studying the patterns on the walls. "According to the scroll, there should be clues embedded in these runes that can guide us to the artefacts."

Nicholas and Zhoha began to decipher the runes, their understanding of elemental magic helping them interpret the ancient symbols. As they worked, the energy in the grotto began to fluctuate, and the whispers of the shadows grew louder.

The shadows coalesced into distinct forms—ethereal beings that seemed to be a manifestation of the vale's protective magic. These beings observed Nicholas and Zhoha with glowing eyes, their forms shifting and changing as they moved.

"We're not alone," Nicholas said, his tone steady but alert. "These must be the guardians of the vale."

One of the shadow beings stepped forward, its voice a low murmur that resonated with the energy of the vale. "Why do you trespass in the Shadowed Vale? What is it that you seek?"

Nicholas stepped forward, his voice firm yet respectful. "We seek ancient artefacts that are said to be hidden within this vale. Our mission is to maintain the balance of the elemental forces, and we believe these artefacts are crucial to our cause."

The shadow guardian regarded them with an inscrutable gaze. "The vale protects its secrets well. If you wish to claim what lies hidden here, you must prove your worth. Only those who truly understand the nature of shadows can succeed."

Zhoha glanced at Nicholas, then back at the guardian. "We are ready to face whatever challenges you present. We are dedicated to preserving the balance of the elemental forces."

The shadow guardian's eyes glowed brighter, and the runes on the walls began to shift, revealing a series of trials. The trials were designed to test their understanding of shadows and illusions, and each one was more challenging than the last.

The first trial involved navigating through a labyrinth of shifting shadows. The walls of the labyrinth seemed to close in and shift, creating a constantly changing maze. Nicholas and Zhoha had to use their knowledge of elemental magic to discern the true path from the illusions.

The second trial tested their ability to control and manipulate shadows. They had to use their magic to create shapes and forms out of shadows to open a series of hidden passages. The shadows seemed to resist their control, making the task more difficult.

The third trial was a test of endurance and perception. They had to remain focused and steady while the shadows around them grew chaotic and disorienting. Their goal was to maintain their composure and decipher a series of hidden messages within the shifting shadows.

Nicholas and Zhoha worked together, using their skills and knowledge to overcome each trial. Their previous experiences and the wisdom they had gained from the scroll proved invaluable as they navigated the challenges.

As they completed the final trial, the shadows around them began to dissipate, and the energy in the grotto seemed to settle. The ancient artefacts, once hidden and protected, became visible on stone pedestals around the grotto.

"These artefacts must be the key to unlocking the next phase of our mission," Nicholas said, approaching the pedestals. "They look ancient and powerful."

Zhoha examined the artefacts carefully. "The scroll mentioned that these artefacts could influence the balance of the elemental forces. We should study them closely and determine their significance."

The artefacts included an intricately carved staff, a crystal vial filled with a swirling liquid, and a series of ancient scrolls covered in enigmatic symbols. Each artefact seemed to radiate its own unique energy, and Nicholas and Zhoha could sense the power within them.

As they examined the artefacts, the shadow guardian reappeared, its form now more solid and less ethereal. "You have proven yourselves worthy. These artefacts are bound to the elemental forces and hold great power. Use them wisely, for they can either aid or hinder your quest."

Nicholas and Zhoha thanked the guardian for its guidance and carefully gathered the artefacts. They knew that these items would be crucial for their continued efforts to maintain the balance of the elemental forces.

With the artefacts secured, they made their way out of the vale, the path now clear and straightforward. The vale's energy seemed to have shifted, and the once-ominous shadows had receded, leaving a sense of calm in their wake.

Their journey to the Shadowed Vale had provided them with valuable insights and powerful tools. As they continued their quest, they were more aware of the complexities of the elemental forces and the importance of maintaining their balance.

Back in their quarters, Nicholas and Zhoha examined the artefacts and studied their properties. The staff, vial, and scrolls each had their own unique attributes and potential uses. The staff seemed to amplify elemental energies, the vial contained a mysterious liquid with transformative properties, and the scrolls held ancient knowledge that could offer further guidance.

"We've made significant progress," Zhoha said, her eyes scanning the scrolls. "These artefacts could play a crucial role in our efforts. We need to understand their properties and how they can be used effectively."

Nicholas nodded. "The artefacts, combined with the knowledge from the scroll, will help us address the remaining challenges. We must continue to be vigilant and prepare for whatever comes next."

Their work was far from over, but with the new artefacts and the knowledge they had gained, Nicholas and Zhoha felt more equipped to face the trials ahead. The journey to maintain the balance of the elemental forces was a complex and ongoing endeavour, but they were committed to their mission.

As they prepared for their next steps, they reflected on the lessons they had learned and the progress they had made. The challenges of the Shadowed Vale had tested their abilities and strengthened their resolve.

With a sense of determination and purpose, Nicholas and Zhoha set their sights on their next destination. The path ahead was filled with possibilities and potential, and they were ready to confront whatever lay ahead with courage and conviction.

The journey continued, each step bringing them closer to fulfilling their role as Guardians and preserving the harmony of the elemental forces. With the artefacts in hand and their knowledge growing, Nicholas and Zhoha were prepared to face the challenges of the future and uphold the balance of the world.

Chapter 14: The Echoing Depths

The weeks that followed were filled with a blend of intense study and meticulous preparation. Nicholas and Zhoha were determined to fully understand the artefacts they had obtained from the Shadowed Vale. Each piece held great promise, but their potential could only be unlocked with careful examination and application.

The staff's intricate carvings seemed to resonate with the elemental energies they had previously encountered. It could channel and amplify these energies in ways they had not fully explored. The vial, with its swirling liquid, was more enigmatic. It had the potential to alter or enhance elemental properties, but its effects were still uncertain. The scrolls were filled with cryptic symbols and ancient lore, which required further deciphering to reveal their secrets.

One evening, as the sun set behind the distant hills, Nicholas and Zhoha sat at a table covered with the artefacts and their notes. The flickering candlelight cast dancing shadows on the walls, creating an atmosphere that was both calming and conducive to their studies.

"Let's focus on the staff first," Nicholas suggested, picking up the ornate weapon. "It's crucial that we understand its full potential. We need to determine how it interacts with the elemental energies."

Zhoha nodded, her gaze fixed on the staff's carvings. "Agreed. We should start by testing its ability to channel the four elements. The scrolls may hold clues on how to properly harness its power."

They began their experiments in a controlled environment, setting up elemental stations with samples of earth, water, fire, and air. Nicholas took the staff and pointed it towards the elemental stations, carefully channelling each energy through the staff. With each test, they observed the staff's effects on the elements—how it amplified, redirected, or transformed them.

The results were fascinating. When Nicholas focused on the earth element, the staff enhanced its solidity and strength, creating a barrier that was almost impenetrable. For water, the staff allowed him to control its flow with incredible precision. Fire responded with increased intensity and reach, while air became more stable and manageable.

"This staff is indeed powerful," Zhoha said, her voice filled with awe. "It can significantly impact the elemental forces. We need to use it strategically to balance and amplify the energies we encounter."

Next, they turned their attention to the vial. Zhoha carefully uncorked it and let a few drops fall into a small, controlled flame. The liquid hissed and shimmered, causing the flame to change colour and flicker with an unusual intensity.

"This vial has transformative properties," Nicholas observed. "It can alter the nature of the elements it comes into contact with. We must be cautious when using it, as its effects could be unpredictable."

They spent the next few days conducting various experiments with the vial, testing its effects on different elements. Each test revealed new properties and potential uses, but also highlighted the need for careful handling to avoid unintended consequences.

The scrolls were the final piece of their puzzle. They meticulously worked through the ancient symbols and inscriptions, slowly unravelling their meaning. The scrolls contained detailed instructions for rituals, spells, and techniques related to the manipulation of elemental forces. They also provided historical context and explanations for the artefacts' creation and purpose.

One particular section of the scrolls caught their attention. It described a ritual that combined the use of the staff and vial to align elemental energies in a specific way. The ritual was complex and required precise timing and coordination.

"This ritual could be the key to stabilising or amplifying the elemental forces at critical sites," Zhoha said, her eyes scanning the intricate diagrams. "We should prepare to perform it at the next significant ley line convergence we encounter."

With their preparations complete, Nicholas and Zhoha set out for their next destination: the Echoing Depths. The Echoing Depths was a cavernous region known for its unusual acoustic properties and elemental anomalies. It was said to be a place where the ley lines converged in a way that created powerful resonances and distortions in the surrounding energies.

The journey to the Echoing Depths was long and arduous, taking them through a series of rugged terrains and treacherous paths. The deeper they travelled, the more the environment shifted, with strange echoes and vibrations guiding their way.

Upon reaching the entrance to the Echoing Depths, they were greeted by a cavernous expanse with walls that seemed to pulse with energy. The acoustics of the cavern created an eerie, otherworldly effect, with every sound echoing and reverberating in unpredictable ways.

"This place is even more disorienting than I expected," Nicholas said, adjusting the staff in his hand. "We need to be cautious and rely on our understanding of the elemental forces to guide us."

Zhoha nodded, her gaze focused on the walls. "We should start by identifying the elemental nodes within the depths. These nodes will help us determine where to perform the ritual."

They ventured further into the cavern, their steps echoing off the walls. The energy in the Echoing Depths was volatile, with elemental anomalies creating fluctuations in the environment. Nicholas and Zhoha used their knowledge and the artefacts to stabilise the energy around them, mapping out the elemental nodes they encountered.

As they explored, they came across several nodes—each representing a different elemental force. Some were stable, while others fluctuated wildly, creating chaotic effects in their surroundings.

"We need to align these nodes to stabilise the overall energy in the Echoing Depths," Nicholas said, examining the unstable nodes. "Let's use the staff and vial to bring them into balance."

They set up their equipment and began the ritual described in the scrolls. Nicholas used the staff to channel and amplify the elemental energies at each node, while Zhoha carefully applied the vial's transformative liquid to modify the energies as needed.

The ritual required precise timing and coordination, with each step affecting the others. The echoes in the cavern became more harmonious as they progressed, indicating that the elemental forces were being brought into balance.

As they completed the final stage of the ritual, the chaotic energy in the cavern began to stabilise. The echoes settled into a rhythmic pattern, and the elemental anomalies were resolved. The cavern's atmosphere shifted from one of tension and unpredictability to a calm and balanced state.

"We've done it," Zhoha said, her voice reflecting a mix of relief and satisfaction. "The Echoing Depths are stabilised, and the elemental forces are now in harmony."

Nicholas looked around the cavern, noting the changes in the environment. "This is a significant achievement. The stabilisation of the Echoing Depths will have a positive impact on the surrounding regions."

With their task complete, Nicholas and Zhoha made their way out of the cavern. The path that had once been disorienting and chaotic was now clear and straightforward. They emerged into the fresh air, their spirits lifted by their success.

Their journey had brought them closer to their goal of maintaining the balance of the elemental forces. Each site they visited and each challenge they overcame strengthened their understanding and their resolve.

As they continued their quest, Nicholas and Zhoha knew that their work was far from over. The balance of the elemental forces was delicate, and their mission required constant vigilance and dedication.

Their path ahead was filled with new possibilities and challenges, but they were prepared to face whatever lay ahead. With the knowledge they had gained and the artefacts they had secured, Nicholas and Zhoha were ready to confront the future with determination and courage.

As they looked out over the horizon, the world seemed to hold its breath, awaiting their next move. With each step they took, they moved closer to fulfilling their role as Guardians and ensuring the continued harmony of the elemental forces. Their journey was far from complete, but with their unwavering commitment, Nicholas and Zhoha were prepared to face whatever challenges lay ahead.

Chapter 15: The Shattered Veil

After the success in stabilising the Echoing Depths, Nicholas and Zhoha were eager to continue their journey. They had learned a great deal about their artefacts and had gained valuable experience from their recent trials. Their next destination was the Shattered Veil, a location mentioned in the scrolls as an area of great significance to the balance of the elemental forces.

The Shattered Veil was known for its mysterious and fragmented nature. Legends spoke of it as a place where the veil between realms was thin and where the elemental energies could be both volatile and unstable. It was said that ancient powers lay hidden within its boundaries, but reaching them required navigating through complex and shifting layers of magical barriers.

Nicholas and Zhoha set out with a sense of purpose, their supplies packed and their minds focused on the task ahead. The path to the Shattered Veil was less defined, marked only by ancient symbols and faded trails. They travelled through dense forests and across rocky terrain, their progress slow but steady.

As they approached the Shattered Veil, the landscape began to change dramatically. The air felt charged, and the sky seemed to shimmer with an ethereal light. The ground beneath them became uneven, with jagged rocks and sudden drops appearing without warning. The atmosphere was thick with magical energy, and the veil between realms seemed to shimmer and ripple.

"This place feels different from anything we've encountered before," Zhoha said, her voice reflecting a mix of anticipation and caution. "We need to be prepared for anything."

Nicholas nodded, his gaze scanning the environment. "According to the scrolls, the Shattered Veil is protected by ancient wards and illusions. We'll need to stay vigilant and use the artefacts wisely."

As they entered the Shattered Veil, they were greeted by an otherworldly landscape. The area was filled with floating shards of rock, suspended in mid-air by some unseen force. The ground below was fractured and unstable, with chasms appearing and closing at random. The entire environment seemed to be in constant flux, making navigation challenging.

"We'll need to find a way to stabilise the area to reach the central point," Nicholas said, studying the shifting landscape. "Let's start by using the staff to channel the elemental energies and see if we can bring some order to this chaos."

Zhoha agreed, and they began to work with the staff, focusing its power on the surrounding energies. The staff's ability to channel and amplify elemental forces was instrumental in creating temporary pockets of stability amidst the chaotic environment. However, the effectiveness of their efforts was limited by the constant shifting of the landscape.

As they worked, they discovered that the floating shards were not just random obstacles—they were part of a larger, intricate pattern that seemed to be guiding them toward a central location. The shards appeared to be aligned with certain elemental forces, and their arrangement suggested a complex, hidden system.

"This pattern must be related to the ancient wards protecting the Shattered Veil," Zhoha said, observing the alignment of the shards. "If we can decipher the pattern, it might lead us to the central point where the ancient powers are hidden."

Nicholas and Zhoha used their knowledge of the elemental forces to interpret the pattern and navigate through the shifting landscape. They carefully moved from one shard to another, using the staff to stabilise their path and the vial to modify the surrounding energies as needed.

As they progressed, they encountered a series of challenges and obstacles. The environment seemed to respond to their presence, with sudden shifts and bursts of energy creating new barriers. At one point, they faced a powerful elemental surge that threatened to destabilise their progress.

"We need to focus," Nicholas said, his voice steady despite the turbulence. "We must work together to maintain control over the energies and keep moving forward."

Zhoha nodded, and they redoubled their efforts. Using the staff and vial in tandem, they managed to overcome the surge and continue their journey. Their understanding of the elemental forces and the artefacts' capabilities proved invaluable in navigating the challenges of the Shattered Veil.

After hours of navigating the shifting landscape, they finally reached the central point of the Shattered Veil. The area was marked by a large, ancient structure—an archway covered in intricate runes and symbols. The archway was surrounded by a field of energy that pulsed with a rhythmic, almost musical cadence.

"This must be the heart of the Shattered Veil," Zhoha said, her eyes wide with awe. "The archway appears to be a key to accessing the hidden powers."

Nicholas approached the archway and examined the runes. They seemed to be a combination of elemental symbols and ancient scripts, forming a complex pattern that required precise alignment.

"We need to activate the runes in the correct sequence to unlock the archway," Nicholas said, studying the patterns. "Let's use the staff and vial to interact with the runes and see if we can unlock the energy field."

Zhoha agreed, and they began the process of activating the runes. Nicholas used the staff to channel elemental energies into the runes, while Zhoha applied the vial's liquid to enhance the connection between the runes and the surrounding energy field. The process required careful timing and coordination, as each rune needed to be activated in a specific order to maintain the balance of the energies.

As they worked, the energy field around the archway began to shift and respond to their actions. The rhythmic pulses of energy became more pronounced, and the runes glowed with an intense light. The archway slowly began to open, revealing a hidden chamber beyond.

"We're getting close," Zhoha said, her voice filled with excitement. "The archway is opening!"

With the final rune activated, the energy field dissipated, and the archway fully opened to reveal the hidden chamber. Inside, they found a large, ancient chamber filled with powerful artefacts and ancient knowledge. The room was bathed in a soft, glowing light, and the air was filled with a sense of profound significance.

"This must be the repository of ancient powers and knowledge," Nicholas said, stepping into the chamber. "We've found what we were seeking."

The chamber contained several artifacts and scrolls, each radiating its own unique energy. The artifacts were similar in nature to those they had previously encountered, but their designs were more elaborate and their energies more potent. The scrolls contained detailed records of ancient rituals and knowledge related to the manipulation of elemental forces.

"We need to study these artefacts and scrolls carefully," Zhoha said, examining the contents of the chamber. "They could provide us with the information and tools we need to further our mission."

Nicholas and Zhoha spent hours exploring the chamber, cataloguing the artefacts and deciphering the scrolls. They discovered that the ancient knowledge contained within the chamber was crucial for understanding the deeper aspects of the elemental forces and their interactions.

"This knowledge could be a game-changer for our mission," Nicholas said, his voice filled with determination. "It will help us address the more complex challenges we face in maintaining the balance of the elemental forces."

With their exploration complete, Nicholas and Zhoha carefully gathered the artefacts and scrolls, preparing to leave the Shattered Veil. They had uncovered valuable information and powerful tools that would aid them in their quest.

As they made their way out of the chamber and back through the shifting landscape of the Shattered Veil, they reflected on their journey. The challenges they had faced and the knowledge they had gained had brought them closer to fulfilling their role as Guardians of the elemental forces.

Their path ahead was still filled with uncertainty, but they were more prepared than ever to confront the challenges that lay ahead. With the new artefacts and knowledge at their disposal, Nicholas and Zhoha were ready to face whatever the future held.

As they emerged from the Shattered Veil and looked out over the horizon, they knew that their journey was far from over. The balance of the elemental forces was a delicate and ongoing endeavour, and their mission required continued vigilance and dedication.

With a renewed sense of purpose, Nicholas and Zhoha set their sights on the next phase of their journey. The world was full of possibilities and potential, and they were ready to embrace whatever challenges and opportunities lay ahead. Their commitment to preserving the harmony of the elemental forces was unwavering, and they were prepared to face the future with courage and resolve.

Chapter 16: The Veil's Wrath

Nicholas and Zhoha barely made it out of the collapsing chamber. Their breaths were ragged, and their pulses raced as they navigated the unstable terrain of the Shattered Veil. The chaotic energy surged around them, distorting the environment and making their escape perilous. The shadowy figure's ominous warning echoed in their minds, a dark reminder of the challenges yet to come.

The ground beneath their feet trembled, sending shards of rock and waves of energy rippling outward. Nicholas clutched the staff tightly, using its power to stabilise their footing, while Zhoha applied the vial's liquid to counteract the surges of unstable magic. They moved swiftly, their path lit only by the erratic pulses of energy that surrounded them.

"We need to find a way out of this place before it consumes us," Nicholas shouted over the roaring noise. "The energy is becoming more volatile by the second."

Zhoha nodded, her eyes scanning the shifting landscape for a possible exit. "Look for any sign of a stable path or a way to navigate through the chaos. We can't stay here much longer."

As they advanced through the Shattered Veil, the environment continued to warp and shift. Floating shards of rock collided with each other, creating explosive bursts of energy that threatened to send them tumbling into chasms below. The rhythmic hum of the chamber's energy field was replaced by a discordant symphony of chaos.

"We're almost to the edge," Nicholas said, his voice strained as he struggled to maintain control over the staff's power. "Just a little further, and we should be able to find more solid ground."

Suddenly, a massive shockwave erupted from the centre of the Shattered Veil, sending a powerful blast of energy hurtling toward them. Nicholas and Zhoha braced themselves as the shockwave hit, nearly knocking them off their feet. The blast created a new fissure in the ground, widening the gap between them and their escape route.

"Hang on!" Zhoha shouted, grabbing Nicholas's arm as they struggled to keep their balance. "We need to find another way around!"

Nicholas gritted his teeth and used the staff to create a temporary barrier against the energy surge. "I see a possible path on the left. It's narrow, but it might lead us to safer ground."

They veered left, navigating a precarious ledge that jutted out from the fractured landscape. The path was treacherous, with shifting rocks and unstable footing making each step a challenge. The shadowy figure's voice continued to reverberate through the energy field, adding to the mounting sense of urgency.

As they pressed on, the energy surges grew more intense, and the landscape became increasingly hostile. The floating shards of rock spun around them in a wild dance, and the ground beneath them seemed to pulse with a malevolent force.

Finally, they reached a more stable area, though it was still far from safe. The Shattered Veil's chaotic energy had settled into a low, ominous hum, but the environment remained unstable. Nicholas and Zhoha paused to catch their breath and assess their situation.

"That was too close," Nicholas said, wiping sweat from his brow. "We need to regroup and plan our next move."

Zhoha nodded, her expression grim. "We have the artefacts and scrolls, but the shadowy figure's warning implies there's more to this than we anticipated. We need to understand what's really at stake here."

As they began to examine their surroundings, a chilling realisation dawned on them. The Shattered Veil, though temporarily stabilised, was still reacting to their presence. The ground continued to shift, and the air was thick with residual magical energy.

"We need to analyse the artefacts and scrolls we retrieved from the chamber," Nicholas said, looking at the items they had carefully packed. "There might be clues about the true nature of the danger we're facing."

They set up a makeshift camp in a relatively secure spot, using the staff to create a protective barrier around them. Nicholas carefully unpacked the artefacts and scrolls, while Zhoha began examining the texts.

The scrolls contained complex rituals and ancient knowledge related to the manipulation of elemental forces. Nicholas focused on deciphering the symbols and inscriptions, while Zhoha scrutinised the magical properties of the artefacts.

"Some of these artefacts have powerful residual energies," Zhoha said, holding up one of the more elaborate items. "They might be key to understanding the forces at play here."

Nicholas nodded, studying the scrolls. "There's a recurring theme in these texts about a 'Veil's Wrath'—a term used to describe a cataclysmic event caused by the imbalance of elemental forces. It seems that our actions in the Shattered Veil may have triggered something significant."

As they delved deeper into the texts, they discovered a passage describing a ritual that could potentially control or counteract the Veil's Wrath. The ritual required a precise alignment of elemental energies and the use of specific artefacts they had encountered in their journey.

"This ritual could be our only chance to prevent further destabilisation," Nicholas said, his tone urgent. "But it requires perfect synchronisation and the proper conditions."

Zhoha glanced at the unstable environment around them. "We need to find a way to create those conditions and perform the ritual before it's too late. The longer we wait, the more the Shattered Veil's energies will spiral out of control."

As they prepared for the ritual, the ground beneath them began to tremble again. The Shattered Veil's instability was increasing, and the chaotic energy surges were becoming more frequent. Nicholas and Zhoha worked quickly to set up the ritual, using the staff and vial to channel and stabilise the elemental forces.

Just as they were about to begin the ritual, a sudden, blinding flash of light erupted from the centre of the Shattered Veil. The energy surge was so intense that it momentarily obscured their vision, and a deafening roar echoed through the air.

Nicholas and Zhoha shielded themselves, their hearts pounding with fear. When the light subsided, they saw a massive rift tearing open in the ground, emanating a dark, swirling energy that threatened to engulf everything in its path.

"That's it!" Zhoha shouted, her voice barely audible over the roar. "The Veil's Wrath is manifesting!"

Nicholas's face was set in grim determination. "We have to complete the ritual now! It's our only chance to contain the rift and restore balance."

With the ritual components in place, Nicholas and Zhoha began the complex process of aligning the elemental energies. They used the staff to channel the forces and the vial to adjust the energy flow, trying to counteract the destabilising effects of the rift.

The ritual required precise timing and coordination, and the chaotic energy around them made it difficult to maintain focus. As they worked, the rift's dark energy surged and pulsed, threatening to overwhelm their efforts.

"We're almost there," Nicholas said, sweat streaming down his face. "Just a little more!"

Suddenly, a massive wave of energy erupted from the rift, pushing Nicholas and Zhoha back and causing the ritual components to scatter. The rift's energy surged uncontrollably, creating a vortex of darkness that began to consume everything in its path.

"No!" Zhoha cried out, reaching for the scattered components. "We have to finish the ritual!"

Nicholas and Zhoha struggled to regain control, fighting against the overwhelming force of the rift. The dark energy seemed to have a mind of its own, resisting their efforts to stabilise it.

As the rift continued to grow, Nicholas and Zhoha found themselves on the brink of being swallowed by the darkness. Their progress was slow, and the energy surges were becoming more violent.

In a desperate move, Nicholas focused all his energy into the staff, creating a powerful surge of light that temporarily pushed back the dark vortex. "Zhoha, finish the ritual! I'll hold it back as long as I can!"

Zhoha nodded, her face determined. She worked quickly, using the vial to stabilise the energy flow and complete the ritual. The process was excruciatingly slow, and the rift's energy was growing more chaotic by the second.

Just as Zhoha was about to complete the final step of the ritual, a blinding flash of light erupted from the rift, and the chamber was engulfed in darkness. Nicholas and Zhoha were thrown violently backward, their vision obscured by the overwhelming surge of energy.

When the light and darkness finally subsided, they found themselves in a completely different location. The Shattered Veil was gone, replaced by a vast, empty expanse of darkness. The rift had disappeared, and the energy surges had ceased.

Nicholas and Zhoha looked around, disoriented and exhausted. They had managed to escape the immediate danger, but the full extent of the Veil's Wrath was still unknown.

"What just happened?" Zhoha asked, her voice filled with a mix of relief and concern.

Nicholas shook his head, trying to piece together their situation. "I'm not sure, but it seems we've been transported somewhere else. We need to regroup and figure out our next move."

As they surveyed their surroundings, they saw a faint, flickering light in the distance—a potential beacon or source of information. With no other clear options, Nicholas and Zhoha headed toward the light, their minds racing with questions and uncertainties.

Their journey had taken an unexpected turn, and the stakes had never been higher. The Veil's Wrath was far from over, and new challenges awaited them in the unknown expanse they now faced.

As they approached the flickering light, they couldn't shake the feeling that they were walking into a new and potentially more dangerous chapter of their journey. The light's uncertain glow seemed to pulse with an otherworldly energy, hinting at both hope and peril.

Part Two

About the Author

My name is Kishan Heraman, and I am a 17-year-old who has spent his entire life growing up in Brampton, a city that has shaped both my dreams and my resilience. From a young age, I've encountered numerous hardships and obstacles, each of which has molded me into the person I am today.

Brampton, with it's vibrant mix of cultures and its own unique set of challenges, has been both a playground and a battleground for me. The journey hasn't always been easy. I've faced personal struggles and external challenges that have tested my resolve and commitment. Whether it was dealing with the pressures of school, navigating complex family dynamics, or grappling with self-doubt, each hurdle has taught me invaluable lessons about perseverance and grit.

Despite these difficulties, my passions have always been my guiding light. I've been deeply committed tomusic, writing, sports, etc... and these pursuits have provided a sense of purpose and direction in my life. Through the trials and tribulations, I've found solace and inspiration in these activities, allowing them to fuel my determination to overcome the obstacles in my path.

My journey is far from over, and I know that the road to success is filled with both challenges and triumphs. But with each step forward, I am learning, growing, and inching closer to my goals. My experiences in Brampton have instilled in me a strong sense of resilience and a belief in the power of hard work and dedication.

I am excited for what the future holds and remain hopeful that, despite the obstacles, my journey will lead me to success in the passions I hold dear.